Nicki wondered how a hallucination could be this real.

Prince Charming was wearing a tuxedo and holding out an engagement ring that he said belonged to her.

"It's real," Garrett said, as if sensing her disbelief.

"Could—you—pinch me?" Nicki heard her voice squeak.

Garrett froze. Surely the woman didn't want him to pinch her, but she looked as if she was going to faint.

"Please."

As the woman's face went whiter, the green of her eyes grew deeper. Like emeralds, he finally decided. Deep pools of muted emeralds. A man could be pulled into those eyes and drown before he knew it.

He slipped the ring back in his pocket and reached out to pinch her, but found himself holding her arms instead. He couldn't pinch her if he wanted. Not through the thick robe she wore. But he had to do something.

So he kissed her.

Books by Janet Tronstad

Love Inspired

An Angel for Dry Creek #81
A Gentleman for Dry Creek #110
A Bride for Dry Creek #138
A Rich Man for Dry Creek #176
A Hero for Dry Creek #228

Silhouette Romance

Stranded with Santa #1626

*Dry Creek

JANET TRONSTAD

grew up on a small farm in central Montana. One of her favorite things to do was to visit her grandfather's bookshelves, where he had a large collection of Zane Grey novels. She's always loved a good story.

Today, Janet lives in Pasadena, California, where she works in the research department of a medical organization. In addition to writing novels, she researches and writes nonfiction magazine articles.

A HERO FOR DRY CREEK

JANET TRONSTAD

Love Inspired

Published by Steeple Hill Books

STEEPLE HILL BOOKS

Steeple
Hill®

ISBN 0-373-87235-6

A HERO FOR DRY CREEK

Copyright © 2003 by Janet Tronstad

Visit us at www.steeplehill.com

Printed in U.S.A.

It is a good thing to give thanks unto the Lord....

—Psalms 92:1a

Dedicated to the princess in our family,
Aurora Borealis MacDonald,
currently four years old.
May all her dreams come true.

Chapter One

Nicki Redfern didn't believe in fairy tales. Instead of glass slippers she wore cowboy boots—and not the highly polished ones rodeo riders wore. No, her boots were sturdy, working boots meant for riding horses and chasing cattle.

Her feet sweat in those boots.

Still, recently, in the early-morning hours while she was lying in her twin-size bed—as the pink sun rose over the Big Sheep Mountains and shone through her small second-story window—her dreams turned to fanciful things such as waltzing with princes and blushing with love.

In the full light of day, of course, Nicki stopped those kind of daydreams. No good would come of them.

A woman like her had no time for Prince Charming or ballroom dancing. She was a farm woman with calluses on her hands and responsibilities on her shoulders. Unless Prince Charming knew how to pitch hay bales, she had no use for him.

When her father died last year, Nicki and her brother, Reno, had inherited equal shares of the Redfern Ranch. The ranch was four thousand acres of prime grassland, starting at the bottom of the Big Sheep Mountains and spreading south to the gully that each year guided the spring run-off into the Yellowstone River just east of the small town of Dry Creek, Montana.

The ranch had been in the Redfern family since 1890 and Nicki was fiercely proud of its history. But it took every ounce of energy from both her and Reno just to keep it going. The price of cattle dropped each year and the dry spell hitting Montana didn't seem like it would end anytime soon.

Nicki needed a hired hand, not some fairy-tale prince.

Besides, Nicki had a weary suspicion that those fluffy dreams were meant for her mother—they had just arrived over twenty years too late. When her mother had left, she'd taken the family honor and eight hundred dollars from the church building fund with her.

Nicki shook her head. There was no point in remembering the woman who had deserted them. No one got everything they wanted in life, and Nicki had learned to be content with what she had—a father, a brother and some of the best ranch land in Montana.

When her father tried to show her some newspaper clippings her mother had sent once, Nicki refused to read them. One look at the accompanying picture of her mother dressed as a Vegas dancer was all Nicki needed to see.

Nicki was half-asleep as she limped down the stairway in her old chenille bathrobe to start the coffee. She was alone in the house this morning. Reno had left yesterday with a truckload of steers. The final cattle sale in Billings fell the day before Thanksgiving each year, and the Redferns always saved their best stock for this sale because the cattle were at their heaviest by then and the buyers more inclined to pay higher prices.

Her brother hadn't wanted to leave her alone. Reno never liked going to Billings and the tumble Nicki had taken yesterday only gave him another reason to fret about leaving the ranch. Nicki had to assure him repeatedly that she was all right. Her horse, Misty, had stumbled into a gopher hole, tossing Nicki to the ground. Nicki was so relieved that Misty hadn't broken any legs that she didn't pay much attention to the bruise coloring her own thigh. Nicki's leg was sore and she couldn't walk far if the old cattle truck Reno was driving had trouble. She'd only slow Reno down if there were problems, and they both knew it.

Nicki yawned as she limped into the kitchen. She headed for the chipped enamel sink and put the nearby coffeepot under the cold water faucet. The sink in the kitchen was right under the window that looked out of the front of the old ranch house. She'd looked out that window thousands of times in her twenty-nine years of life. She always saw the same thing—the old oak tree that had the rope swing dangling from its branches and the mountains in the distance.

It was still more night than day outside. Nicki looked out the window wondering if it would be light enough to see the rope on the tree. The swirl of snowflakes made it especially dark outside. She could only see outlines and pinpricks of white snowflakes. Actually, it was the snowflakes that made her look twice.

She blinked and then closed her eyes before blinking again.

Whoa—the man didn't disappear like she'd thought he would.

He was right there, standing like a figure in a darkened snow globe. The man was looking at the house and leaning against the side of a long, white limousine—a limousine so unexpected and shiny, it could as well be a pumpkin carriage sprinkled in fairy dust.

And the man! She only saw the outline of the man, but he looked…well, wonderful. Magical. A white scarf was wrapped around his neck and dangled down over a black jacket that looked suspiciously like a tuxedo. Nicki's eyes followed the man's long legs all the way to the ground and then back up again because there was Hunter, Reno's half-wild dog, standing politely at the man's side.

Nicki had to blink. Oh, my word! Nicki woke completely.

Prince Charming! She was looking at Prince Charming. And he was apparently there with a limousine to take her away to the royal ball.

The cold water ran over the sides of the pot and chilled Nicki's hand. She slowly set the pot down in the sink and turned the water off.

She kept staring. The man didn't fade.

She told herself it was time to sit down before she lost it all together. Limousines didn't appear in the driveway of the ranch. Neither did Prince Charming. As for Hunter, the dog would never calmly stand beside a stranger.

Nicki was hallucinating. Her mind had somehow reached into her dream and pulled out the image that had been filling her nights. That much was obvious. She couldn't remember hitting her head when she'd catapulted off Misty yesterday, but she must have done so. What else could explain this?

Nicki stumbled over to a chair.

She needed to stay calm. She'd close her eyes for a bit and wait for it to grow lighter outside. She didn't want to wake Dr. Norris this early. She'd be fine. She'd sit a minute before she tried making coffee again.

And, in the meantime, she'd try to pray. Her father had stopped going to church when Nicki's mother left, but he had still insisted on driving Nicki to services in Dry Creek. So every Sunday Nicki sat in the same pew her family had occupied before her mother left. She sang all the hymns and joined in all the congregational prayers.

But, in private, Nicki never prayed. If she thought about talking to God, no words came. Even now, instead of talking to God, she stared at the bare lightbulb hanging from the kitchen ceiling and started to talk to it. *Oh, my, I think I could use some help here… It's not possible—I know it's not. But I'm seeing Prince Charming standing outside my window! Do you think I'm crazy?*

Garrett Hamilton liked the cold of the morning as the snow settled in damp patches on his face. The weather was bracing. And at least when he was standing outside the limousine he didn't feel so much as if he were in the middle of a bad prom date. Nobody but an aging Vegas dancer would insist he wear a tuxedo uniform to fill in for her sick chauffeur, especially when he was doing her a favor.

Well, technically he was doing the favor for his cousin, Chrissy. Or was it his aunt Rose who was responsible for him being here?

"Yeah, it had to be Aunt Rose," Garrett said to the dog who stood silently and watched him. He'd been talking to the dog for a good hour now, and he'd swear the animal understood. "Aunt Rose got me into this one."

Garrett had resisted Aunt Rose's worries about her daughter, Chrissy for weeks now. But that last conversation had gotten to him. She'd said Chrissy had asked him to come.

Garrett snorted. The dog whimpered in agreement and Garrett nodded. "Yeah—I should have known better."

Chrissy hadn't asked him to come, especially since she knew Aunt Rose wanted him to find out more about what was going on with Chrissy and her boyfriend. "Can't say I blame her. Don't know what Aunt Rose was thinking. Shoot, I don't know what I was thinking."

Garrett looked down at the dog.

When Garrett had cut the engine on the limousine and let it coast into the driveway of the ranch late last night, the dog had been there. When Garrett opened the window, the dog moved out of the black shadow under the tree and growled low and deep in his throat. Garrett knew the dog wouldn't give much further warning if Garrett were foolish enough to just open the door and step out of the limousine.

It was too dark for the dog to see whether or not Garrett was looking at him directly, but Garrett knew the dog could sense any fear and would use that as a trigger to attack. Even as the dog growled, Garrett admired the animal. The dog had a torn ear and a scar along its left flank. ''You've had a hard time, haven't you, Old Boy?''

Garrett knew that the way to settle a wild animal's nerves was to give him time to get used to you. So he took his old leather coat, the one that he sometimes wore for sixteen hours at a stretch when he was on a long haul, and gently threw it out the window for the dog to sniff. After the dog scratched at the coat and rolled it around in the snow, the dog seemed resigned to Garrett's scent. Not happy, but at least not growling anymore.

''That's a good dog.'' Garrett knew how the dog felt. Sometimes, even if you got used to something, you still might not like it much.

That's how Garrett felt about this mission his aunt had sent him on. Aunt Rose meant well, but if she hadn't been able to convince Chrissy not to marry her high school sweetheart, Garrett wasn't likely to, either. Besides, Garrett would rather have a tooth pulled than see Chrissy cry. This gave Chrissy a tactical advantage that she used shamelessly.

Garrett was the last person who should give marriage advice anyway. He knew he wasn't a family man.

Garrett was even more of a mutt than the dog beside him. Garrett's mother had died when he was five. After that, alcohol had been all the family his father needed. Garrett had raised himself and, while he had no complaints, he knew less about being a family man than the dog beside him did.

Which was all right.

"I've got my life and it's a good one." Garrett was a legend among truckers. He'd set a record from New York to San Diego that hadn't been broken yet. "A man can't ask for more than that." Garrett loved all that asphalt rolling under his wheels. There were plenty of strangers along the highways and not one of them gave Garrett any grief.

Giving him grief had become Aunt Rose's job. The odd thing was Garrett hadn't even known his aunt Rose until his father died and she showed up at the hospital. She'd told him then that she wanted to adopt him and have him come to live with her and Chrissy, but the thought of being part of any real family had scared Garrett spitless. He told Aunt Rose he'd do fine on his own, and he had.

Garrett wouldn't admit it, but he had grown fond of Aunt Rose over the years. They had made their compromises. She no longer expected him to spend any holidays with her and Chrissy. But they had their own tradition. Every September after Labor Day Garrett came to spend a few days with Aunt Rose and Chrissy. He'd clean out the rain gutters and do any heavy chores they needed. Plus, no matter where he was, he made it a point to pull off the road on Saturday at three in the afternoon and make sure his cell phone was on. That's when Aunt Rose would call.

Aunt Rose didn't ask much more of him than that and so, when she'd asked him to talk to Chrissy, he'd known she was desperate. What could he say but yes?

He should have had his head examined.

Chrissy had flatly refused to talk to Garrett when he pulled into Las Vegas. All she needed, she said, was a favor. Garrett had agreed to help her before he even knew what she was going to ask.

"Bad habit of mine," Garrett mentioned to the dog before glancing back at the limousine just to be sure the woman his cousin had asked him to drive to Montana was still sleeping on the long back seat. Chrissy had met Lillian at the casino where they both worked—Chrissy as a waitress and Lillian as an entertainer. ''I thought she was going to ask me to move some furniture in the back of my truck or something. I could move a whole city block in the back of Big Blue.''

Garrett had already told the dog about Big Blue. Garrett's fourteen-wheel big rig was now parked near the casino where Chrissy worked. The dark blue cab had Hamilton Trucking stenciled in white lettering on the door. It wasn't the fanciest rig on the highways and it certainly wasn't the newest, but Garrett knew Big Blue and he had confidence in her.

Garrett looked back at the ranch house. Surely someone would be up soon. He thought he'd seen some movement at that window, but then he'd looked closer and decided he'd imagined it.

He felt a stirring of sympathy for the poor man who lived inside. The man had no idea what a surprise this morning would bring. Garrett's passenger had asked him to go to the door and prepare the man for her arrival.

From the few remarks the older woman had made and the engagement ring she'd asked him to return, Garrett figured Mr. Redfern had wanted to marry the woman at one point in time and didn't know she was coming to visit.

A visit like this could give an old man a heart attack.

Failing that, it could give Garrett one.

"Ah, here we go." Garrett relaxed.

Someone had turned a light on in the kitchen.

The morning sun still had not made its way completely over the mountains so Nicki didn't risk looking out the window this time. She focused on filling the pot with water. Once that was done, she'd start the coffeemaker and sit down again. It was a good thing she didn't have many chores to do today.

The knock on the kitchen door came just as the pot was filled with water. Nicki calmed herself. No need to panic. She told herself that the still falling snow had muffled the sound of someone driving up. It must be Lester.

Lester Wilkerson was her neighbor—and friend, Nicki added to herself somewhat guiltily. The fact that he made her nervous wasn't his fault. So far she'd managed to derail most of his hints about getting married, but he didn't seem discouraged.

Nicki figured she would eventually marry Lester, but she just needed more time to get used to the idea. She had no illusions about why Lester was interested in marrying her. His land ran along the east side of the Redfern Ranch, and he had his eye on more grazing area for his cattle.

Nicki knew some people wouldn't see that as a good reason to get married. But Nicki preferred it to some nonsense about love. Land stayed with a person. Love, on the other hand, could fly away at any time.

Lester didn't expect love and neither did Nicki. They would suit each other well. And things between them would be better once they actually got married. Nicki hadn't been able to bring herself to meet Lester's lips yet when he attempted his clumsy kisses, but she supposed she'd come to accept him before long.

In the meantime, Nicki expected Lester would continue his plodding courtship. He had started going into Dry Creek early every morning to pick up the mail for both ranches and then coming over to have coffee with her and Reno.

Yesterday morning Lester had bought her a lavender orchid in a plastic box. The petals were waxy and the flower felt artificial even though it was real. Still, it was a sensible flower for snowy weather in Montana and Nicki appreciated that. The brief yearning she'd had in her heart for roses was easily stamped down. She was a practical woman and should be pleased with a practical flower. Roses wouldn't last long here.

Nicki flipped the switch on the coffeemaker before she wiped her wet hands on her chenille robe. She limped over to the door and looked out the small window. All she could make out through the frosted glass was the general shape of a man.

It had to be Lester on the other side of that door, but Nicki wasn't fool enough to just open it for anyone unless she was ready.

She looked over by the ancient refrigerator. There it was. Reno had bought a thick-handled broom at a farm auction last year. Then he had taught her how to hit with it. They were both thinking of that stubborn cow's head when she practiced her swing, but it'd stop a man as quick as a cow. She brought it over.

Nicki unlocked the door and opened it.

Her jaw dropped and she stared.

If it had been the Boston Strangler on the other side of the door, she wouldn't have been able to raise the broom in defense of herself.

It was him. Prince Charming. Flakes of snow sparkled in his hair. He sparkled everywhere. His teeth sparkled. His eyes sparkled. Even the shine on his shoes sparkled. But, as much of a fairy-tale prince as he appeared to be, one thing was clear. "You're real."

Chapter Two

Garrett waited for the woman to finish her sentence. He thought she was going for "real cold" or maybe "real lost." Even "real strange" would do, but the sentence just hung in the air.

Garrett looked past the woman into the kitchen of the house, but he didn't see anyone else there. Having a woman answer the door certainly complicated things. He'd assumed Mr. Redfern was an old bachelor or maybe an old widower. The woman he'd brought up here wouldn't welcome the presence of another woman, especially not someone twenty years younger than her.

"Good morning." Garrett cleared his throat.

The woman still stared at him.

Garrett looked at her. She seemed dazed. Maybe

she was a little slow. He softened his voice. "Sorry to bother you, but I'm looking for your husband."

The woman's eyes widened and her voice squeaked. "My husband?"

Nicki began to realize something very important. Prince Charming was standing on her porch talking about husbands and she hadn't combed her hair. Or washed her face. Or put on any clothes except her ratty old robe. Oh, my, she was a mess.

"I can wait for him outside. I'm sure you'll be more comfortable with him around."

"He's not—" Nicki breathed. "I mean, I'm not married."

This is where the music starts, Nicki thought to herself. Her heart literally tingled. She'd been wrong all those years. Fairy tales did come true. Forget about her boots. Forget about that waxy orchid in her refrigerator. They didn't matter. Her world had shifted on its axis because Prince Charming was here. Any second now he was going to hold out his arms to her and she was going to float away into some beautiful fairy-tale land where totally impractical rose petals would softly fall on them as they waltzed together. Just like in her dreams.

The prince frowned. "I must have the wrong place," he said, and then turned to walk away.

Nicki gasped. This wasn't how the story was supposed to end. The prince didn't just leave before one rose petal even had time to fall. "It's cold. It'll only take a minute for you to warm up inside."

Nicki stepped back so the man could come into the kitchen.

Prince Charming didn't go into the kitchen, but he came close enough to the door to feel the heat. Nicki forgot to breathe. Outside, the shadows and half-light of the morning had hidden all but the outline of the man's face. But up close in the light she'd turned on in the kitchen—well, his nose and chin were classical; his eyes were a smoldering pewter; his raven hair was thick and wavy. And there—when he smiled— was a deep dimple in his chin.

Nicki was staring. She knew it. But all she was able to do was stand there leaning on the open door as the man stood on the porch. Even the cold wind blowing into the house didn't make her move.

Nothing could make her move—and then she heard the slam of a car door.

"Garrett," a woman's voice called out in exasperation. "Garrett—where are you?"

Nicki's heart sank when "Garrett" turned in response to the woman's call.

Nicki looked out the open door and saw...*her.*

The woman was wearing one of those glamorous wide-brimmed hats so Nicki couldn't see her face but, even without seeing the woman's face, there was no mistaking the fact that she was beautiful. Blond and svelte—with enough gold draped around her neck to bankroll a small kingdom.

Why was it, Nicki thought, that when Prince Charming finally showed up on her doorstep, he had Cinderella in the car with him?

Nicki's eyes looked down at the woman's feet. Yes, the woman was Cinderella right down to her tiny little feet perched on some ridiculously high-heeled shoes that did little to protect against the snow.

Nicki expected the man to go to the woman, but he didn't. She heard Hunter's low vibrating growl as the woman walked closer, but the dog didn't leave the man's side. Garrett put his hand down and rested it on Hunter's head. The dog stopped growling. "Maybe you could tell me how to get to the Redfern Ranch. I'm looking for Mr. Redfern."

"Reno?" Having a stranger ask for her brother was almost as shocking as seeing some unknown man silence Hunter with a touch. The dog never let anyone touch him except Reno.

"No, it's Charles Redfern I'm looking for."

"My father is dead."

"Oh. Are you sure? Mr. Charles Redfern?"

"Of course I'm sure."

"Garrett," the woman from the car called out to the man.

"Your friend—" Nicki had to look around the

man to see the woman from the limousine ''—she sounds angry.''

''I'll get to her in a minute.'' Garrett reached into his pocket and pulled out the diamond ring that the woman insisted belonged to Charles Redfern. The ring had found one of the holes in the pocket of Garrett's uniform and it kept falling out at the most awkward times like last night when he was talking to that kid in the café, getting directions to the ranch. Garrett wanted to be rid of it. The woman before him was the man's daughter. That was enough for him. ''This ring belongs to you now, I guess.''

Nicki stared at the ring. It was a delicate ring with one small center diamond and a circle of fiery opals around it. She heard the sound of the woman muttering angrily, but Nicki didn't turn to look again. She couldn't be bothered with Cinderella.

Nicki wondered how a hallucination could be this real. But it must be a hallucination. The man was wearing a tuxedo and holding out an engagement ring that he said belonged to her. And something about the memory of it made it seem as if he was right.

''It's real,'' Garrett said, as if sensing her disbelief.

''I—I don't think—'' Nicki heard her voice squeak. Oh, my. ''Could you—could you—pinch me?''

Garrett froze. Surely the woman didn't want him

to pinch her, but she looked as if she was going to faint.

"Please."

As the woman's face went whiter, the green of her eyes grew deeper. Like emeralds, Garrett finally decided. They were like muted emeralds. Deep pools of muted emeralds. A man could be pulled into those eyes and drown before he knew it. She really was quite…unusual. But still. "I can't pinch—"

He thought she was going to faint.

He slipped the ring back in his pocket and reached out to pinch her, but found himself holding her arms instead. He couldn't pinch her if he wanted to. Not through the thick robe she wore. But he had to do something.

So he kissed her. On the lips.

He meant it to be a pinch of a kiss. Just a peck to say he hoped she didn't faint. But she gasped, and he—well, he forgot why he was kissing her. He just knew that he was experiencing the sweetest kiss he'd ever shared with anyone. He didn't want it to end.

Nicki couldn't breathe. She'd never been kissed by a hallucination, but she figured it couldn't be like this. She really thought she'd have to faint after all.

"Oh, for Pete's sake, I'll pinch her!" The woman's annoyed voice penetrated Nicki's fog just before she felt the sleeve of her robe being raised.

Cinderella used her nails to deliver a solid pinch.

"Ouch!" The fog left Nicki instantly. She was definitely not hallucinating.

Nicki looked up at the man. He looked dazed. But the petite woman standing beside him had lifted the brim of her hat and didn't look the least bit vague.

Oh, my. Nicki suddenly wished desperately that she was dreaming after all. The woman's hair was bleached so blond, it shimmered in the faint morning light. Her lips pouted a well-penciled pink. Diamonds dangled from her ears and hung from her graceful neck. The woman looked like she was forty, but Nicki knew that she would turn fifty-five this coming May 13.

"What are you doing here?" Nicki said the words. They sounded defensive to her own ears. But then, she decided, she was entitled to be defensive. The woman hadn't even written in twenty-two years. If it wasn't for the photos in the news clippings that came in the mail periodically, Nicki wouldn't even recognize her now.

The woman's jaw lifted slightly. "You must be the housekeeper. I came to see Mr. Redfern. Would you tell him I'm here?"

Nicki wished with all her heart that she had gone with Reno into Billings. She could have crawled home if the truck had broken down. The woman standing before her didn't recognize her, but Nicki would know the woman's face anywhere. It appeared life really wasn't a fairy tale, after all.

Nicki opened the kitchen door farther. "Maybe you should come inside."

Nicki let the woman walk in front of her and enter the kitchen, but she didn't follow her. She needed to wait.

Nicki forgot she was still holding the end of the broom handle until she felt it pressing against the length of her thigh. That meant it was not only pressing into Garrett's leg, it was also resting on his foot. "I'm sorry, I— my brother makes me use this when he's not here."

Nicki and Garrett were standing facing each other in the middle of the doorway to the kitchen. The main door swung out over the porch, letting cold air come in. The screen door swung back into the kitchen, letting warm air seep out. Neither one seemed able to move.

Garrett's ears were ringing. He decided it must be the altitude. His ears felt as if they were stuffed with cotton, as well. "Huh?"

"The broom. He wants me to carry it." Nicki told herself she was barely making sense. She was feeling a little dizzy. But it was only natural. She needed more than a minute to think before she faced her mother.

"Whatever for—?"

"So I can hit heads." Nicki knew she should step aside so they could close the kitchen door, but she was afraid her legs wouldn't work. She'd just stand where she was for a bit more. She needed to focus on the man's face instead of the woman in the kitchen. No, his face wasn't a good thing to look at, either. How could a man be so sexy that even his Adam's apple made her wobbly?

"You want to hit me? On the head? You'll need a stepladder."

Nicki looked up and saw in surprise that it was true. The man was a good six inches taller than herself. It wasn't often that a man was that tall. "You're supposed to be a cow."

"I beg your pardon?"

"I'm supposed to hit the cows' heads with the broom handle. Just on the forehead. To show them which way to go."

"I see," Garrett said. He seemed bewildered as he put his hands around the broom handle so she didn't drop it.

"It doesn't hurt them," Nicki added. She let the broom fall into his hands. Now, why did she have to tell the man something like that? He'd think she was a barbarian. Not that his opinion mattered. He was only her mother's— Nicki stopped herself. Just who was the man in her mother's life anyway?

"Have you known her long?" Nicki jerked her

head in the direction of her mother. She could hear her mother inside the kitchen as she walked across the floor to the counter where the coffee was.

The hostility in this woman's voice cut through Garrett's haze and reminded him the other woman was Chrissy's friend. "Long enough. And you?"

Nicki gave an abrupt laugh. "Me? I barely knew her."

The wind had blown snow across the wooden porch. Nicki could see white puffs coming out of her mouth when she talked. She could feel the goose bumps on her arms, and the frozen boards of the porch chilled her feet even though she had her winter slippers on. She was used to the weather in Montana and she was still cold. "She won't want to stay for long so you might as well go inside and get warmed up. It's freezing out here."

Garrett nodded. The cold would explain the tingling he still felt all over his body. Yes, that would be it. And his breathing. That would explain why his breath was coming hard. But as the woman backed up farther against the doorjamb, all he could think about was that she had to be even colder than he was. "You go ahead—you must be freezing. You're in your pajamas."

The sun was rising and the day was taking on a faint pink glow. Garrett couldn't help but notice how delightful the woman's face was when she blushed.

"It's a robe."

Nicki had never wished for silk in her life until now. Her chenille robe must be twelve years old. It had been faithful and warm, but it was not what a woman dreamed about wearing at a moment like this.

Not that, Nicki assured herself, it would matter for very long. The man in front of her would be leaving with her mother and, if Nicki had anything to say about it, that would be happening soon. Nicki pulled on the ties of her robe to knot it more securely. She was a sensible ranch woman. She didn't need silk. She didn't need her mother. She didn't need some fantasy prince. She had her land, her boots and her pride. That had to be enough.

Garrett looked at the woman. The cold had turned her nose red and the wind had blown strands of her hair this way and that way until they finally just gave up and tangled around her head. Her hair was neither permed nor colored nor highlighted. She kept it brown—not honey-brown, not mahogany-brown. Just plain brown. And she didn't have a dab of lipstick anywhere.

Added to that, she was wearing an old bathrobe that kept her shape so well hidden, a man couldn't tell if she was a woman or a fence post.

Still, she appealed to him in a crazy sort of way. Garrett wondered if the snow could have frozen his brain or something. The woman sure wasn't the usual kind who caught his eye. He liked a woman who strutted her stuff and wore her clothes tight enough so a man didn't have to strain himself wondering what was underneath.

And that robe wasn't his style. He liked the black see-through kind that was worn more for invitation than for warmth. The bulky old robe this woman wore wouldn't get her noticed in a monastery.

Besides, the robe said loud and clear that the woman who wore it was a nice woman who wasn't inviting anybody to look at her twice.

Garrett made it a policy to stay away from nice women because they always thought a man like him had promise. It wasn't true, of course, but try convincing a woman who was intent on reforming him. If he knew one thing about himself, it was that he was a short-term kind of a guy. He liked the freedom of the road. Given that, he felt it was only right to keep his dating to women who weren't interested in a long-term arrangement, either.

Granted, Garrett had grown a little tired of dating strangers lately. He told himself he was just off his game. He hadn't been out on a date in six months.

But that was bound to change soon. Somewhere, someplace, a woman in black spandex was waiting for him.

Still, if he had been the sticking-around kind of guy, there was something about this woman that interested him even more than the black-spandex ones. Maybe it was the freckles on her neck. She'd tied the belt of the robe tight around her waist and that made the collar bulge just enough so he could see the light sprinkling of freckles that scattered out from her collar bone. The bone itself was fragile and made him feel protective. But it was the freckles that were his undoing.

For the first time in his life, Garrett wished he knew a thing or two about marriage.

"I'm sorry, I—" Garrett began. He didn't know what he was going to apologize for exactly. Maybe the fact that cold air had gone into her warm kitchen. Or that he had snow on his shoes. Or that he hadn't been born into an Ozzie-and-Harriet kind of a family.

Nicki shifted in the doorway. A faint pink made her face glow in embarrassment. The man didn't need to apologize. She wasn't such a ninny that she thought he was serious. Of course, she was acting like one. The man had been making her agitated and that wasn't like her. She was usually very calm and sensible.

"I know it wasn't a real kiss." Nicki waved her hand vaguely, as though she'd experienced a million kisses that were real and so could tell the difference instantly. "You don't need to apologize."

Garrett frowned. "What do you mean it wasn't a real kiss?"

"That's what I'm saying—it wasn't like the kiss was supposed to be real, so you don't need to apologize."

"I wasn't apologizing for kissing you."

The pink on Nicki's face deepened. "Oh, well, I just wanted you to know I know it didn't mean anything. It was just because of the ring, and me asking to be pinched and you in that tuxedo and all."

"It's not a tuxedo, it's a uniform. Besides, every kiss means something."

Nicki could hear her mother's high-heeled footsteps as she continued walking from the counter that held the coffeepot to the counter that held the dishes. "Where do you keep the cups?" her mother called out.

Nicki forced herself to turn and look. Everything in the house looked shabbier than it had when her mother left. Because of her fall yesterday she hadn't even done the dishes from yesterday. Three mugs stood around the sink. "There are more mugs in the cupboard."

Every Christmas the hardware store in Dry Creek gave away a mug to its customers with the store's name on one side of it and the year on the other. In addition to the three by the sink, another dozen of those mugs sat in the cupboard.

Nicki's mother took one look at the dirty cups. "I'm not talking about mugs. I'm talking about real cups. I always drink my coffee from a real cup. Something pretty and tasteful. Surely, Charles still does the same.''

''I'm afraid the mugs are all that we have.'' Nicki tried to hold back the defensiveness in her voice, but she didn't succeed. Nicki wasn't sure she wanted the woman in front of her to realize that she was her daughter. The fuss the woman was making over cups that were functional instead of pretty only reminded Nicki of how critical her mother had been of her. Nicki had never been the pretty little girl her mother wanted. Nicki remembered that her hair never curled enough and the lace on her dresses always made her itch so she couldn't wait to change into her jeans.

''But these mugs don't even match.''

''They don't need to match to hold coffee.''

All of a sudden, Nicki realized what her mother was looking for. Nicki's mother had had a set of English bone china that served sixteen, but Nicki and Reno kept it packed away in the old bunkhouse where their father had put it. The dishes were the one thing Nicki hadn't even dreamed of replacing over the years. Her mother loved that china with its clusters of pink roses and the gold rim around each plate.

Nicki decided she needed to get the mugs so that her mother could drink her coffee and leave. She forgot about her leg, however, and her first step made her wince.

"You're hurt!" Garrett said, and stepped toward her. Unfortunately, he let go of the broom handle so that he could steady Nicki just as she moved again. Instead of falling to the floor harmlessly like it should have, the broom landed on Nicki's foot.

"Oooh." Nicki felt the pain shoot up through her leg. The broom hit her toes and her slippers weren't enough of a cushion. To make matters worse, it was her good foot that had been hit. The bruise was on her other leg and so now she didn't have one good walking foot between the two legs.

The dismay on the man's face made Nicki wonder if her face had turned white with pain. "Don't worry. I'll be fine. It's just that yesterday my horse fell and now this—"

"You need to stay off your feet," he said.

"I'm fine. Really." Nicki gathered the collar of her robe around her more closely. To prove she was all right, Nicki carefully put one foot in front of the other and started walking toward the cupboard that held what dishes they did have. She smiled to show it didn't hurt.

Her smile turned to gritted teeth as she bit back the moan. Oh, my, that hurt.

"It's my fault the broom fell," Garrett said as he stepped forward and scooped Nicki up in his arms.

Nicki gasped in surprise. Maybe she was still dreaming. Her cheek was pressed against the tuxedo's satin lapel. The suit even smelled of class. Nicki wished she were wearing perfume. Forget perfume—she wished she were at least wearing deodorant.

''You need to put me down. I can walk,'' Nicki said. But maybe she couldn't walk. Everything seemed dizzy. Her whole world was shifting. Her heart was building up to a pounding close to thunder. Being swept up by Prince Charming was a fantasy come true.

Nicki's mother walked closer to the two of them and frowned. ''Are you Mrs. Hargrove's daughter? You look familiar.''

Nicki kept her cheek pressed against the man's shoulder.

''Doris June? No, I'm not her,'' Nicki answered when she knew her mother couldn't see her eyes. Doris June Hargrove had gone to school with Nicki. She lived in Anchorage now and was working for a television station there.

''Oh, I was just wondering.'' Her mother didn't sound convinced. ''I'm sure Charles needs someone to look after the house for him since both of the kids took off like they did on him.''

''Who told you anyone took off?'' Nicki asked quietly when she was finally sitting on the kitchen counter. She reknotted the tie on her robe just so she had somewhere for her eyes to focus that didn't involve looking at her mother.

"Why, Charles, of course. He wrote me a letter. Years ago. I'd written to ask about the kids, and he said they'd just up and left. I was surprised about that, but I suppose they had their reasons. He promised he'd let me know if he found out where they were. Have you worked for Charles long?" Nicki's mother smiled thinly. "I know I'm going on, but I would like a cup of coffee before I have to see Charles. Do you think he'll be up soon?"

"No, no, he won't be up soon," Nicki said. Everything seemed fuzzy. Her whole world was shifting. Her heart was pounding. She didn't know whether it was because of seeing her long-lost mother or because she'd woken up to see Prince Charming.

Nicki immediately rejected the idea that her mother could affect her like this. She'd gotten used to living without a mother and she was doing fine. The woman standing by the sink could be any woman. Nicki didn't feel anything for her.

Not that, she remembered with a start of guilt, she should be so willing to think the dizziness was from the man, either. She shouldn't be swooning over any man. She was going to marry Lester. That thought alone was enough to bring her back to earth with a thud. At least it settled her stomach.

"Oh," Nicki's mother said as she turned to leave the kitchen. "If he's not going to be up soon, I'm going to visit the ladies' room while you finish making the coffee. It was a long drive."

"The bathroom's upstairs," Nicki offered. "The first door on your left."

"I remember where it is."

Nicki didn't say anything as she listened to the staccato tapping of her mother's heels as she climbed up the stairs.

Garrett wished he could offer to clean out the rain gutters on this woman's house or something. She looked drawn and pale, and he'd always had a soft touch for any wounded being. Of course, it hadn't helped anything that he had dropped the broom that hit her foot. And the broom wasn't half-plastic like the ones they made today; it was pure oak and could do some serious damage. "Let me look at your toes."

"What?" Nicki looked up in time to see Prince Charming reaching for her slippers.

"I'm hoping no toes are broken."

Nicki was just hoping she'd survive.

Garrett had never seen more elegant feet. The toes themselves were worthy of a poem. "I like the pink."

Nicki blushed. She had never meant for anyone to see the nail polish on her toes. She didn't want to wear polish on her fingers, because someone was sure to comment on that. But she figured her toes were safe from the eyes of others and a good way to practice using nail polish just in case she ever wanted to do her fingernails. "There's nothing wrong with having good toe hygiene."

Nicki almost groaned. She was sounding like a schoolteacher. No wonder there had never been a line of men waiting at her door to date her. "I'll be fine in a minute. My foot will be better."

"I'm sorry I dropped the broom."

The man didn't need to apologize, Nicki thought. A man that good-looking—women probably flocked to him to have their toes bruised. It must be the tuxedo, she decided. That, and the way he had of lifting her into his arms, as though she didn't weigh any more than a feather.

Nicki wondered why Lester had never swept her off her feet like Prince Charming here had done. She might mention it to Lester. That's right, she told herself. It was the action that had made her heart all jumpy. It had nothing to do with the man. If Lester put on a tuxedo and swung her up into his arms, she'd feel the same breathlessness as she felt now. She might even want to kiss Lester after something like that.

Nicki heard a motor in the driveway. "I'd better get down four mugs."

Seeing Garrett's bemused expression, Nicki said, "Lester's here." She reached for the mugs and put them down on the counter beside her.

"And who's Lester?"

Nicki hesitated. "Our neighbor. To the east of here."

Nicki told herself she didn't owe this man any explanations. "He's just here for his coffee. Oh, and some coffee cake."

Nicki started to brace herself to slide off the counter.

"No, you don't." Garrett stepped over and held out his arms to scoop her up again.

"You shouldn't."

"The floor's cold."

Nicki nodded. She supposed once more wouldn't hurt. It might actually be a good thing. She probably wouldn't be dizzy this time, and she'd know it had only been a momentary thing before. It was really for scientific research that she was going to let Garrett carry her again.

Nicki slid into his arms.

Garrett was a happy man. The fuzzy material of Nicki's bathrobe brushed against his cheek and the pure soap smell of her surrounded him.

"You didn't need to carry me. I can walk if I have to."

Garrett knew that. But he wasn't fool enough to

pass up the opportunity to carry her again. He'd even walk slow. The refrigerator was way across the kitchen. If he worked it right, he could almost make a waltz out of the whole thing.

Nicki heard Lester's footsteps on the porch. Fortunately, the door was already unlocked. "Come on in."

Garrett felt the cold air rush into the kitchen, but that's not what made the back of his neck tingle. Something was wrong. He heard the door slam. It was followed by the quick hissing indrawn breath of an angry man.

"What the—?" The bellow coming from the doorway made Garrett turn as the man charged toward him. The man was small, but wiry—and red enough to explode.

Garrett had been in enough street fights as a kid to know what was coming, but he'd never had someone in his arms before. If he had even a second longer, he could have slid Nicki down to the floor. But the man was coming too fast. All Garrett could do was protect her as best he could. He pivoted so that Nicki was not between him and this madman.

"Lester," the woman squealed.

Garrett only had time to bend his shoulder so he could hide Nicki in the hunching of his shoulder. The man's fist caught him high on the right cheek.

"Lester!" Nicki tried to twist out of Garrett's

grasp so she could slide down to the floor and get her broom. What had gotten into him? She'd always assumed Lester was shy and that was why he was so patient with her about kissing and things like that. But the man in front of her wasn't shy. He was acting like a deranged man. "Stop that! What do you think you're doing?"

Garrett's hands held her to him like steel.

"What do I think I'm doing?" Lester exploded. Garrett wondered how the vein in the man's head could throb that hard. "Just what do you think you're doing here with some man and you in your night-gown?"

Ah, so that's the way the story went, Garrett thought to himself. Well, he supposed the woman had to have a boyfriend. Even in a remote area like this, the men would be foolish not to notice the— Garrett stopped himself. It wasn't beauty he noticed. It certainly wasn't stylish clothes. What was it about the woman?

"I've got a robe on—not just my nightgown," Nicki corrected him. "And if you'd bothered to no-tice, you would see everything is perfectly innocent and—" she could hear her voice rising "—just what do you think is going on anyway?"

Nicki had lived by the rules all her life. Lester should know that.

Lester flushed. He was so red already that he actually grew less red when he flushed. Now he looked mottled as he mumbled. "Duane at the café told me some guy stopped last night at midnight and asked how to find the Redfern place. Some guy in a tux. Everyone knows Reno took those steers down to Billings and that you're here alone."

"What's Reno got to do with—?" Nicki stopped and then realized what he was implying. "Lester Wilkerson, you have your nerve!"

Garrett felt the swelling start on his cheekbone. He hadn't had a bruiser like this since he'd stepped between two fighting truckers once. He supposed it was safe for Nicki to slide down to the floor now, but Garrett didn't want her to leave his arms. Some primitive part of him figured he was entitled to carry her now that he'd taken a fist to his face on her behalf.

Nicki heard her mother's footsteps as she came back down the stairs.

"Did I hear something about Reno?" Nicki's mother stood in the doorway and asked. "Reno still lives here?"

Everyone in the kitchen forgot Nicki's nightgown and the bruise on Garrett's cheek.

"Let me get you your coffee." Nicki slid to the floor and tested her foot. Garrett let her rest against him until she was steady and then she stepped away. "I put the clean cups on the counter."

"Why would Reno be here? Charles said the kids

had both left.'' Nicki's mother walked over to the counter. ''He said he would let me know if he heard from them.''

By now the older woman had picked up one of the clean mugs Nicki had put on the counter and was rubbing the side of it almost unconsciously. She had stopped smiling and her face seemed to age ten years as she stood there. ''I know Charles was angry with me. But if Reno's here and he didn't tell me, that's not fair. When Charles wakes up, I'm going to have to tell him that's not right.''

Nicki felt her face was so tight, it would rip. She refused to cry in front of this woman. ''There's nothing you can tell him. He's dead.''

The woman dropped the cup and no one noticed. ''Oh, dear.''

For the first time since she'd recognized her mother, Nicki had a glimpse of the woman her mother used to be. ''I'm sorry. I shouldn't have blurted it out like that.''

''No, no—'' Nicki's mother waved the apology away. ''I just wasn't expecting this is all. Does Nicki know? Did anyone find her to tell her? She'd want to know.''

''She knows.'' Nicki swallowed. She'd never thought herself to be a coward, but she found that the words to tell her mother who she was wouldn't come without forcing.

"But—" Lester started to speak until Garrett put his hand on the man's arm to silence him.

Nicki looked at both men. There was nothing to do but say it. "I'm Nicki."

Nicki wished her mother had another cup to drop. Anything would be better than the silence that greeted her announcement. The other woman just stared at Nicki.

Nicki reminded herself that she didn't need fairy tales, not even ones that involved mothers coming home again to their daughters.

"Well—" Nicki finally found her voice. The silence was unnerving. "Let me pour you some coffee before you go."

Nicki was proud of the fact that her face didn't crumble. No tears came to her eyes. Even the anger was gone. She would give her mother a cup of coffee and that would be that.

Nicki didn't even limp as she walked toward the coffeepot.

Chapter Three

Garrett was losing his touch. He would have bet Big Blue that Lilly would melt into a puddle of sentimentality at the fact that her daughter was standing before her. Aunt Rose would have been crying into her tissue by now.

But the woman stayed dry-eyed. He thought her hands trembled and her face did grow paler, but she certainly wasn't smiling with joy. She looked over at Garrett. "We're going to have to leave. I didn't know she was here."

Garrett felt a clutch in his stomach at her words. Something was going on here and he had a feeling it was something worse than anybody's sore toes. He took a step closer to Nicki just in case she needed him.

"I'm in the room. You can talk to me," Nicki said as she gripped the handle on the cup she had pulled from the dish drainer.

"Oh, dear— It's just that I'm surprised. Your father's letter said— Well, I just didn't expect you to be here," Lillian said as she walked over to the sink.

Garrett knew people didn't always say what they meant the first time around. He turned to Lillian. "Maybe if you told her why you're here. Surely there's a reason."

The older woman hesitated. "I just came to see Charles, that's all."

The man's question brought Nicki back into focus. Why was her mother here? Nicki turned to face the woman. If you took away the powder and the makeup, you could see traces of the woman she had once been. "You could have come to see him years ago."

The clock ticked and the old refrigerator gurgled.

"And what's he doing here?" Lester finally spoke and jerked his thumb at Garrett.

"I'm Garrett Hamilton. I'm a trucker. I drove Lilly Fern up here."

"And why did you come again?" Nicki turned from the man and addressed her mother.

"I came to talk to your father," Nicki's mother said defiantly. "There's no harm in that."

"You can't possibly think he would want to see

you now even if he were alive. You left him years ago.''

"He was my husband. I never did divorce him.''

"That's it? You came to ask him for a divorce after all these years?''

"Of course not. I don't need a divorce.''

"Then what is it—is it money?''

Lillian laughed. "Charles never had any money. All he ever had was this ranch of his.''

"He loved this ranch—'' *And he loved you.* Nicki almost said the words and then choked them off. What did it matter now?

Lillian wasn't even looking at her any longer. "I know we can't always go back, but I have unfinished business in Dry Creek and I needed a place to stay for a little bit—''

"You're in trouble?''

Lillian shrugged. "In a way, I guess.''

"And you need a place to hide?'' Strangely enough, Nicki was relieved. Her mother really hadn't come looking for her father because she missed her father or had any fondness for him. She'd just come looking for a safe harbor in some storm she was facing.

"Your father would want me to be here now. He'd feel he owes me that much.''

Nicki felt her world click back into place. Everything was as it had been. It felt good to know her way around once again. The fact that her mother had come to her father hoping for comfort in some crisis didn't surprise her. Her father never turned away anyone in need. He might not talk to them much, but he'd let them stay.

"Nobody here owes you anything." Nicki wasn't her father.

"Don't worry. I couldn't possibly stay here now anyway." Lillian Redfern reached out her hand for a cup of coffee. "Once I've had a cup of coffee, Garrett will drive me back to Dry Creek and we'll stay there for a few days."

"Dry Creek?" Nicki didn't like the sound of that.

Garrett wasn't sure he liked the sounds of it, either. He frowned. "No one said anything about days. I thought we were planning to leave tonight." Garrett planned to be in Las Vegas tomorrow night so he could pick up Big Blue and hit the highway.

Lillian looked up at Garrett. "I'm sure you won't mind. It's just going to take longer than I thought."

Garrett did mind, but he didn't have time to speak up before Nicki was talking.

"You can't just stay. Not around Dry Creek," Nicki said.

"No one would deny a widow the right to stand by her husband's grave."

"You're going to tell them you're going to the cemetery?"

"Of course. And I will be. It's the respectable thing to do. I have a black dress with me. I always travel with at least one black dress. And I'm sure someone in Dry Creek will let me stay with them."

"After what you did when you left?" Nicki's hand shook ever so slightly as she poured another cup of coffee into a hardware store mug. "I wouldn't think you'd be very welcome."

Lillian sat down at the kitchen table and took a sip of coffee. "Oh, yes. The money. I suppose they still remember that."

Nicki looked at her mother incredulously. "Of course they remember the money. You stole over eight hundred dollars from the church building fund. I don't know how many bake sales the women of the church had. How could you possibly think they might have forgotten?"

Lillian smiled slightly. "I thought they might have had other things on their mind at the time." Lillian took another sip of coffee and then looked at Nicki. "My leaving was hard on you, wasn't it?"

"No. I did fine."

Nicki could feel Lester looking at her. She glanced up at him. Even now that he was calm, he looked odd. She'd never seen him look like this. His face looked blotched. But he was her Lester. She could count on him. "Haven't I done fine?"

Lester grunted and jerked his thumb at Garrett.

"You're sure you don't know him? Jazz at the café said he had a ring and everything ready to propose."

Garrett felt his heart stop. He'd thought the teenager had looked at him strangely when the ring fell out.

Garrett cleared his throat and looked Nicki in the eye. "You did just fine. I can tell."

Nicki was annoyed. Lester should have been the one to say that. "Thank you, but you don't know me well enough to judge."

Garrett grinned. He rather liked the vinegar look on Nicki's face. "It's early. I've got time."

"What's he talking about?" Lester mumbled.

"Oh, for Pete's sake, he's not proposing," Nicki said firmly as she smiled at Lester and glared at Garrett. This was all Garrett's fault. Everything had been fine—until he came up here. Who went around carrying an engagement ring and wearing a tuxedo in the middle of Montana farmland? No wonder poor Lester was confused. "Look at him. He's not even from around here."

Garrett frowned at that. "Good people come from other places, too."

Nicki took a deep breath. "What I meant is that you don't know me and I don't know you so there's no reason to think you'd be proposing. We're strangers."

"I've seen your toes."

"What's he talking about? And what's he doing here anyway?"

Nicki wondered why she'd never seen Lester like this before. What had happened to his hair? She hadn't noticed how his light brown hair was starting to thin and the pink of his scalp showed through, making him look old. And when he squinted like that, his eyes made him look like a ferret. Maybe it was only the cold weather that had scrunched up his face like this. She'd need to get him a warm cap for Christmas. That's what she'd do, she thought. A warm cap would make him look better.

"He brought me here," Lillian said graciously to Lester. "I don't believe we've met. Were you here when I was around? I'm Nicki's mother."

Lillian held her hand out to the man.

Lester had his hand halfway out to meet hers and he stopped in midair. "That's what Nicki's talking about—I remember hearing about you—you're the one who stole the church's money?"

Nicki saw her mother's polite smile tighten. "Is that what they say about me?"

"Yes, ma'am," Lester agreed doubtfully.

"Well, then, I'm getting off easy, I guess."

"Well, I don't know about that—taking money is pretty serious."

"Well, they'll just have to forgive me," Lillian said firmly. She lifted her chin up slightly. "Once an apology is given, it is their Christian duty to forgive.''

Lester looked at Lillian, frowning slightly. "I must have missed hearing about the apology."

Nicki could have gone to Lester and hugged him. Now this was the Lester she knew. Unswayed by flattery. Polite and logical, with his feet firmly planted on the earth and no hint of sentiment about him. Not at all like Prince Charming who stood looking at her like she needed some kind of rescuing.

"Well, I haven't given an apology yet," Lillian admitted with a hint of reproach in her voice. "I haven't even finished my coffee." Lillian took a slow sip from her cup. "What do you suppose they'll say?"

"What do you mean?" Nicki felt a small ball of dread starting to roll around in her stomach.

"Why, when I go into Dry Creek and apologize, of course."

"You don't really need to apologize," Nicki said. The last thing she wanted was for her mother's name to again be the primary topic of conversation for Dry Creek. "That's all over and done with."

"I can't do that. You two convinced me of that." Lillian nodded at Lester. She took another sip of coffee. "I can't have people saying I didn't apologize."

"You could write a note," Nicki offered in desperation. People never got as worked up over a letter as they did when someone talked in person. Besides, who knew what her mother would say when she opened her mouth. Nicki could correct a letter.

"What kind of a lady would write a note about something like that?" her mother asked.

The same kind of lady who would steal from the church on the way out of her children's lives, Nicki thought, but she held her tongue.

"No, I'm right," Lillian said firmly. "I'm going to apologize and put an end to all of this. All I need to do is find the minister of that little church. We'll all drive into Dry Creek and find him."

"All of us?" Lester shuffled his feet and looked at Nicki before glancing at Garrett. "You're sure that guy's not proposing?"

"Absolutely."

"Then I'm going to get back to my place. I still have some cattle to feed."

"I could come help you," Nicki offered.

Lester brightened. "You could?"

"She's coming with me." Garrett interrupted them. It was one thing for Nicki to reassure the man that no one was proposing to her, it was another to run off for a cozy drive with her boyfriend while she left her mother with Garrett.

"Nicki and Garrett will take me to Dry Creek," Lillian said airily, as if she was in charge. "They won't need anyone else."

Lester looked at Nicki and shrugged before heading toward the door.

Nicki tried again. "It's early morning. The minister won't be up yet."

"Then we'll wake him up," Lillian said as she stood. "It's his duty to hear confessions."

"You're thinking of priests." Nicki groaned. "Priests hear confessions."

"Priest, minister, it's all the same," Lillian said as she adjusted her skirt and turned to Garrett. "Would you mind bringing the car closer to the door this time? The snow is so slippery and in these shoes—"

Garrett could tell from Nicki's face that her Lester had disappointed her when he made his exit without her. Garrett shouldn't be happy about that fact, but he was. To make up for it, he turned to Nicki and asked, "How about it? Would you like me to bring the car closer so you don't have to walk in the snow?"

"Me?" Nicki breathed lightly. Her Prince Charming was worried about her feet. That's when she remembered she was in her slippers. "Oh, I can't go. I'm not dressed."

Nicki had been searching for a reason not to go, and when she found one she realized she was oddly disappointed.

"Well, I can't leave you here." Garrett didn't want to drive Lillian back into Dry Creek all alone.

"And put on a dress, darling," Nicki's mother called out as she walked toward the kitchen door. "We have time for you to look nice."

Nicki couldn't believe she was hearing those words again. The only time Nicki had worn a dress since her mother left was to her father's funeral. And she certainly wasn't going to wear that dress for her mother's return, Nicki told herself as she limped up the stairs again.

Nicki did have some nice pants outfits that she wore to church. She pulled one of them off its hanger before she reconsidered and hung it back up. No, she wasn't going to fall into the trap of trying to please her mother.

Instead, Nicki put on the jeans she generally used to muck out the barn. They were clean, but they didn't look it. She topped them off with an old sweater of her father's. Her mother might not like it, but Nicki didn't care.

She didn't want to hear what her mother said about dresses and looking good, anyway. Nicki knew she was hopeless. She only had to look in the mirror to know she wasn't princess material. Her mother had been as delicate as the lily that gave her its name. But there was nothing delicate about Nicki's face. She had her father's square jaw and determined forehead. Her hair was plentiful and shiny, but it never took on the styled look that some women's hair had. She just kept it cut and tied back out of her face.

There was never any reason to fuss with her hair. The cows didn't care. Reno wouldn't notice. Even Lester wouldn't care.

Nicki decided her mother would have to accept her as she was.

Nicki felt foolish the minute Garrett opened the passenger door of the limousine for her. She felt like a rebellious Cinderella who had declined her fairy godmother's offer of new clothes but had gone to the ball anyway. The interior of the car was sleek—if it was proper to call the limousine a car. It looked more like an ocean liner to her eyes. Nicki had never seen such a long length of leather that wasn't attached to a cow. And there was a small refrigerator. And her mother.

"Maybe I should drive the pickup in to Dry Creek and just meet you there," Nicki suggested softly as she looked up at Garrett. "I don't really know that I should ride in here dressed in jeans—"

Garrett shrugged. "You can ride up front with me if you'd like. It's not so fancy up there."

Garrett told himself that Nicki was just like any other woman he'd taken for a drive. Any kind of breathing problem he'd had after that kiss had only been because of the freezing temperature.

"I do have a dress," Nicki said when Garrett turned the heater on inside the limousine. The defroster slowly blew a clear space on the front window. "I should have worn it. I imagine all of the women in Las Vegas wear dresses."

Of course they wore dresses, Nicki told herself. Sexy black dresses that pleased men more than mothers.

Garrett grunted. "I'm not from Vegas."

"Oh. I just thought that since Lillian was from there—" Nicki turned her head and noticed the glass window that separated the driver's area from the rear of the limousine was firmly closed. At least her mother and Garrett hadn't been chatting away cozily.

"I don't know your mother. I'm just doing a favor for Chrissy."

"Oh." Of course there was a Chrissy in his life. Or a Suzy or a Patti. Some petite blonde with style. A man that good-looking wouldn't be alone. "I see. Well, good for you."

"I don't know about that."

"Well, of course it's good. And I'm sure she appreciates it."

"She'd better. If she doesn't I'm going to tell her mother about it."

"You're good friends with her mother, too?" Nicki smiled stiffly. The man was practically married whether he knew it or not. "That's nice."

"Well, it's my aunt Rose. Chrissy Hamilton is my cousin."

"Oh."

Nicki decided she should look for something else to wear when she was in Dry Creek. Really, the only store in town was the hardware store, but the stock had changed so much since the minister's new wife, Glory, was doing the ordering that maybe, by some magical coincidence, there were dresses hanging on a rack by the farmer's overalls.

The window separating the front of the limo from the back opened and Nicki smelled a trace of her mother's lily perfume.

"She's getting married, you know. Chrissy is," Lillian announced. "It'll make her mother proud."

"It'll make her mother mad if Chrissy doesn't invite her," Garrett said.

"You can hear back there what we're saying?" Nicki wondered what the point of having a window like that was if it offered no privacy.

Her mother didn't even bother to answer her. "Chrissy said there was no need for anyone to come to her wedding."

Nicki thought about her own mother. "I expect Chrissy has her reasons for not inviting her mother."

Garrett snorted. "Well, if she does, she'd better get them spelled out in a letter or something. And mighty quick. Aunt Rose is a force to be reckoned with when it concerns her family. I should know.''

Garrett still remembered the determined look on Aunt Rose's face when she met him at the hospital the day his father's liver finally gave out and he died. Garrett was quickly learning something about the forms that needed to be filled out when someone died.

Garrett hadn't even finished half of the forms before Aunt Rose came to the hospital and took over. She'd told him he wasn't alone in this world as long as she was around and she was going to take him home to live with her and Chrissy. Garrett had already made arrangements to stay in the house where he and his father had lived, but he was touched. Not many single mothers would take on a belligerent sixteen-year-old nephew who knew more about hospital forms than college applications.

''Oh, I'm sure Chrissy will have some pictures taken.'' Lillian shrugged. ''And maybe a video. Some of the chapels include a video with the service. Chrissy's mother can watch that. It'll almost be the same thing.''

''Aunt Rose won't think so. She's still hoping Chrissy will go home for Christmas and get married in the living room where she grew up.''

Nicki wondered what it would be like for someone to want to be at your wedding that bad. She supposed

Reno might be upset if he wasn't invited to her wedding. Of course, he would also be relieved since he hated any public gathering. "Do you think Chrissy will do that?"

"Not likely."

"Well, I think Christmas would be a lovely time to get married. Or even Thanksgiving," Lillian said as she leaned closer to the partition that separated the back from the front. "Too bad she won't be up here tomorrow. Thanksgiving was always my favorite time on the ranch. All those pies we used to make."

"We don't do Thanksgiving at the ranch anymore," Nicki said curtly. Who was her mother trying to fool? It almost sounded as if there was some nostalgia in her voice.

"Really? For the first years I was gone I used to picture you and your father and Reno sitting down to these big Thanksgiving dinners. You know how your father used to like to have the table bulging with food and half the families in Dry Creek coming over to eat with us. There'd be the Hargroves. And the Jenkins. And, of course, Jacob and Betty Holmes—"

"We don't have company at the ranch anymore."

"Well, you should—the Redfern Ranch is important to this community. Besides, I was sort of hoping to relive one of those Thanksgivings while I'm here," Lillian said as she leaned back into her seat and her face was no longer in the window. "I can almost smell the turkey now."

"Sounds like you have some good family memories," Garrett said after a minute or two had passed.

Nicki looked up at him in surprise. How could they be good memories when they only reminded her of what she had lost? "All that ended."

"I see."

Clearly the man didn't see at all, Nicki thought to herself miserably. "You wouldn't know what it was like. Reno, Dad and I made peace about celebrating Christmas, but Thanksgiving was just never the same. Last year I made meat loaf."

"Nothing wrong with that. The fanciest we ever got in my family was a can of turkey noodle soup."

"Well, at least you had your family with you."

Garrett grunted. The only reason his father had been with him on Thanksgiving was because the bars were closed in the morning and he was too drunk to walk anywhere else by the afternoon. He liked to start his holiday celebrations early. It was Garrett who heated up the soup.

But Garrett didn't believe in telling people about his past. What was done was done. He was doing fine in life now. Of course, he had spent more Thanksgivings in truck stop cafés than he could count, but there was more to living than eating a plate of turkey on some cold Thursday in November.

Besides, he reminded himself, he liked not having the kind of family ties that meant he had to sit himself down to a Thanksgiving table every year. He was a free man.

Chapter Four

Meanwhile in Las Vegas

Chrissy sat up on the edge of her king-size bed in the Baughman Hotel. Today was going to be her wedding day and it would be a good day if she could only stomp down the nausea that threatened her. Now that she had Garrett hundreds of miles north of here and her mother hundreds of miles south, Chrissy was ready to take her vows.

She'd made the appointment with the wedding chaplain for nine o'clock in the morning so that no one would be hanging around the Rose Chapel in the Baughman Casino.

She knew it was bad luck for the groom to see the bride before the ceremony, but she figured her luck couldn't get much worse. Besides, she was too tired to put on her work clothes just to give a loud wake-up knock on Jared's door. Instead, she slipped on the wedding dress Jared had bought for her.

Chrissy hadn't planned to buy a special wedding dress. She had a gray suit that would have worked fine. Besides, a wedding dress seemed a little expensive under the circumstances. They were saving their money to buy a house, and Chrissy didn't mind scrimping on a wedding if they could find a house sooner.

But Jared had showed up with this dress anyway so she slipped it over her head. She turned to look at the hotel mirror. She looked even worse in it than she feared. The dress was short, strappy and it had some kind of iridescent, glittering sequins sewn on every inch of the fabric.

If she had feathers in her hair, Chrissy would look like a showgirl in it. Which was probably why Jared had chosen the dress. Chrissy looked at the material a little more closely. She hoped he hadn't just lifted the dress off one of the costume racks at the back of the casino.

Chrissy had always dreamed of an elegant ivory wedding gown that would sweep the floor and make her look like one of those brides she'd seen on the covers of magazine racks in the drugstores in Glendale.

All of which just went to show that weddings weren't always what a girl imagined they would be. Sometimes there were more important things to consider.

Jared's room was just down the hall from Chrissy's, and she was surprised to find his door was slightly open. She hadn't expected him to be still up. He'd had his bachelor party last night with a couple of friends, and that was why he was staying in a separate room. He said he didn't want to disturb her when he came in late.

Chrissy wasn't happy about the party, but she had smiled gamely. She didn't like the two guys he hung out with, but she never said anything. When they were married, Jared would be all hers. Jared had promised they could leave Las Vegas then and buy a house in some little town somewhere. Chrissy couldn't wait for that day. She hated the crush of people in Las Vegas. She wouldn't even mind waiting tables so much if she knew some of the customers.

''Jar—'' Chrissy pushed the door open and stopped. At first she thought she must have the wrong room because all she saw was the back of a woman kissing a man. But then she noticed that whoever had his arm around the woman was wearing one of Jared's favorite shirts.

Chrissy told herself there could be hundreds of

shirts in Las Vegas with black spades embroidered on their cuffs. She looked down at the man's shoes.

Then she looked back up at the woman. The woman was wearing Jared's bathrobe.

Shirt. Shoes. Bathrobe.

Chrissy took a step back and stumbled over a high heel that had been left on the floor. Her soft cry made both people turn and look at her.

The woman was one of the casino chorus girls.

"Chrissy!" Jared smoothed back his hair. "You're early."

Chrissy wondered if she should have known Jared had been involved with a woman. She believed in trusting the man she loved. Maybe she'd been too trusting. Had there been signs?

"Just let me get dressed and we'll go downstairs and get married right now." Jared was regaining his voice.

Chrissy held her hand up. "Don't—don't bother. You might as well stay here."

"Don't be silly. You're not going to let a little bit of fun stop us from getting married."

"Yeah, you're all dressed and everything. That's a great dress, by the way. It looks even better on you than me," the blonde said.

Chrissy wondered if the woman was as insensitive as she sounded. She turned to Jared. "You got the dress from her—no, don't answer. Just give me the keys to my car.''

Chrissy had brought her car with her to Vegas. It was her car even though Jared borrowed it most of the time.

''Ah, Chrissy, don't be that way.''

Chrissy took a step back as Jared walked toward her.

''Don't touch me.'' Chrissy hoped the burning in her eyes didn't turn into tears. She wanted to leave with dignity. ''Just give me the keys.''

Jared smiled. ''Ah, don't be mad. Remember, the car's in the shop. They have the keys. It won't be ready until tomorrow.''

''Maybe they'll finish early.''

Chrissy backed out of the hotel room. She'd talk to the mechanic. She needed to leave Vegas and she needed to leave soon. But where would she go? She couldn't go to her mother's. Maybe she could connect with Garrett and Lilly. Lilly had talked about the people in Dry Creek, Montana. That's where she'd go.

Chapter Five

"The café's open," Garrett announced as he slowly drove down the gravel road that was Dry Creek's main street. It was nine o'clock in the morning and just about time for some bacon and eggs in Garrett's opinion. He hoped the café served a hearty breakfast.

Garrett stopped the limousine in front of the café. He had to park parallel to the road because the limo was so long. The café had been lit up last night, and here it was all lit up again this morning. "Somebody puts in long hours."

"That's Linda Evans and Jazz, well, really Duane Edison. He just goes by Jazz—they're trying to raise enough money to buy the old Jenkins' farm. They're very responsible youngsters."

Nicki didn't know why she kept spouting off like an old schoolteacher. It must be because, even with the bruise around his eye starting to swell, she'd never met a man so gorgeous as Garrett. He might have stopped sparkling, but he still made all of her frustrations rise to the surface and scream their heads off. Not that she had any intention of letting him see how he affected her.

No, she'd keep her emotions in tight rein. She could do that. After all, her reaction had nothing to do with him personally. She would be rattled by any man who looked as if he'd been sprinkled with gold dust. Not that a man like that would ever be hers in real life. She was destined for a solid plodding man like Lester, who would be useful on the ranch. That was her future. She needed to be practical and stop dreaming about sparkling princes and men like Garrett.

"Is everybody around here so set on staying?" Garrett opened his door.

Nicki looked up at Garrett like he was speaking a foreign language. "Dry Creek is our home."

Garrett grunted. When he was talking to the dog this morning, he'd wondered if all the people in Dry Creek already had their burial plots picked out. He was beginning to think he'd guessed right when he said yes. That kind of certainty made him itch under the collar. How could a man breathe if he knew every step he'd be taking for the rest of his life?

If Garrett was ever fool enough to marry, it would have to be some poor restless soul like himself. He delayed swinging his legs out of the cab of the limousine. "Don't you ever feel the urge to go other places?"

"I go to Billings."

Garrett grunted again. "Why stop there?"

"That's as far as we need to go for cattle sales." Nicki wasn't sure about going into the café with Garrett. He was dressed in his tuxedo and she had on her barn clothes. "You go ahead. I'm really not very hungry."

"Well, I am." Garrett stepped out into the snow-covered road.

Garrett looked down the long gravel road leading into Dry Creek. For the first time since he could remember, looking at a road made him feel a little depressed. There was something lonely about the thought of one man traveling it all by himself. Garrett decided it must be because he was missing Big Blue. Or maybe he needed to get a dog to travel the road with him so he'd have someone to talk to during the long nights.

Garrett walked around the limousine. Breakfast would make him feel better.

A light sprinkling of snow settled on the front window. Nicki was comfortable in the car watching Garrett until she heard the small window click open behind her.

"I'm glad to see you remember some of what I taught you. A lady never eats breakfast like some ranch hand," Nicki's mother said. "Speaking of which—I hope you're taking care of your hands, too."

Nicki turned to stare at the woman behind her. The woman might be her mother, but Nicki saw nothing of herself in the face that looked through the small window. Her mother's face was like a porcelain doll's. It was flawless, but not real.

"Mother, look at me. I never was the pretty little girl you wanted me to be. I don't have time for lotions and fancy manicures. We need summer help on the ranch, but we don't have money to pay anyone. So, Reno and I do everything. I bale hay and brand cattle. I'm not a lady, I'm a working ranch hand." Nicki opened the door and stepped out. She stood tall and took a deep breath. Nicki knew she was going to order the full stack of pancakes. The morning was beginning to look better.

Garrett already had a foot on the step that led up to the porch that surrounded the café door when Nicki caught up to him. She felt she should caution Garrett about the steps leading up to the café, but she knew Jazz had fixed them all. Maybe it was the door that she should warn him about.

Nicki's heart sank when she heard the woman's voice. Now *that's* what she should have warned Garrett about.

"Oh my, oh my—" Linda shrieked the moment Garrett stepped inside the café. Nicki and Garrett were both just inside the doorway now and Linda saw them. "Jazz said—but, oh, my!"

Nicki knew it was a mistake bringing Garrett to town without a hat on his head to hide his handsome face, but what could she do now?

"This is Garrett Hamilton." Nicki introduced the man beside her. "He's just in town to—to—"

"I know, I know—" Linda squealed. The teenager had a red streak in her hair and a row of silver earrings circling her left ear. She wore a long black dress with a white chef's apron over it. She had a tattoo of a butterfly over her left eye. She was the last person in Dry Creek who should be making a fuss over how someone looked and, if Nicki got her ear privately for a moment, she would suggest that to Linda. "Jazz said—but I never…I mean, I thought he was mistaken or—well, I just never thought." The teenager stopped to take a breath and reached her hand out to Garrett. "Pleased to meet you."

Garrett was beginning to wonder if Dry Creek might be a little too far off the beaten path. Jazz, the young man he'd talked to last night, looked at him oddly and then this young woman acted as if she'd never seen a stranger. "The pleasure's all mine."

Four empty square tables, each with four wooden chairs, stood in the middle of the café. Garrett liked the casual fifties look of the place. The floor was black-and-white linoleum and there were red-checked vinyl cloths on the tables. Each table had a squeeze bottle of maple syrup. That was a good sign. He liked pancakes. "This is a very nice place you have here."

"Oh." Linda turned to Nicki. "And he has such nice manners. That's a good thing in a…well, a—" Linda put her head close to Nicki's ear and whispered "—in a husband."

"In a what?" Nicki was glad her teeth were attached. Otherwise, they would have fallen out of her mouth. She had completely forgotten that Lester had gone on about Jazz seeing the ring the man had.

"Oh, I hope I didn't spoil the surprise." Linda put her hands over her lips. "I shouldn't have said anything. I just thought that by now he would have asked."

"Garrett isn't—" Nicki closed her mouth. Garrett was looking at her puzzled. He hadn't heard what Linda had whispered and Nicki wasn't about to tell him. She came as close as she dared. "That was my mother's old engagement ring. Garrett's just passing through Dry Creek and he returned it. Besides, you know I'm not dating anyone."

Linda lowered her voice so only Nicki could hear. "But you want to, don't you? He's the best-looking man I've ever seen around here. You've got to want to date him."

Nicki blushed and shook her head. "No, I—"

Linda winked at Nicki and turned to Garrett. "Sorry about that. Nicki was just telling me about her latest date with Lester. You probably don't know him—"

"Oh, I know him." Garrett turned so the young lady could see the bruise on the right side of his face. "He gave me this."

"You were fighting." Linda stopped and frowned. "Nicki doesn't like fighting."

"Tell that to Lester."

"Lester started the fight? That doesn't sound like Lester."

Linda moved over so she could whisper in Nicki's ear. "You don't want to marry him if he's always picking fights with people. I don't care if he begs you. Say no."

"I don't need to say no," Nicki whispered back. "He's not asking."

Linda nodded and continued brightly, "Yes, Nicki is almost married to Lester. He's got a big ranch north of here."

"He doesn't care about Lester." Nicki felt her blush deepen. Why didn't Linda just put an Available sign on Nicki's forehead and set her out on the street so every man who drove through Dry Creek could stop and refuse to ask her out?

Linda barely stopped to listen to Nicki. She continued speaking to Garrett. "Lester took her to the Christmas pageant last year. I remember they had the spaghetti dinner here that night, too. Jazz's band was playing romantic music and Lester was very attentive." She shrugged. "It's only a matter of time."

Nicki shook her head. Why did everyone think she needed to be dating? Lots of perfectly fine women didn't date. Of course they were mostly nuns. "Lester doesn't need to ask me on a date. He's a friend of the family. He invited Reno that night, too."

"She's got you there," Garrett agreed cheerfully. "Sounds like a friend-of-the-family dinner instead of a date to me."

"Family's important to Lester," Linda continued. "That's why he invited Reno."

Nicki frowned. She'd never really thought about why Lester had invited Reno. Now that she thought about it, she realized Lester had talked mostly with Reno. Nicki wondered for the first time if she was as boring to Lester as he was to her. They always did seem to run out of conversation after they covered the weather and the crops. Sometimes cattle prices kept them going longer.

It was depressing to realize that the man you were going to marry had nothing to talk to you about and you were halfway through the dating phase. This was supposed to be the fun time.

"What do you think about the weather?" Nicki looked at Garrett and demanded. "You're a trucker. Weather is important. Do you talk about it?"

"I guess so." Garrett shrugged.

"I mean on a date. Do you talk about it on a date?"

Garrett turned to Nicki. The light was coming in the window of the café and it hit Nicki on the cheek. It gave her a golden Mona Lisa kind of a glow. Something was bothering her and, for the first time in his life, Garrett truly wished he understood women.

"No." Garrett hoped this was the right answer. "Unless you do, that is."

"I was afraid of that." Nicki shoved her hands into the pocket of her coat. She'd forgotten all about her hands until her mother reminded her. They weren't the hands of a dating woman. She didn't wear polish. She kept her nails clipped short. And the skin on her hands was rough and sometimes chapped. She was a fool to think for a moment that Garrett would date someone like her. At least a man like Lester wouldn't worry about her hands or her lack of conversation. "I need to get back and help Lester feed the cows."

Garrett didn't know how one man could be so annoying. "I'm surprised Lester doesn't feed them by himself. Or is it some kind of a date in disguise where you sit and talk about the weather and look at the cows?"

"I don't date," Nicki said.

Linda turned to frown at Nicki. "What Nicki means is that she's been too busy to date very much lately."

"What I mean is that I have to get back and get to work," Nicki repeated.

Garrett grunted. So she didn't date. That meant she'd never go out with him, but it cheered him up anyway. "That's too bad. I don't date much, either, these days."

Nicki stiffened. Who was he trying to fool?

The scent of baking biscuits came from what must be the café's kitchen. Garrett breathed in. "That smells good. Can I put in an order for some of those biscuits with some eggs and bacon?"

Linda thought a moment. "The early rush wiped us out. You're welcome to wait but it will be a few minutes. Will that be a table for two?"

"No, we'll need a table for three."

Lillian was still in the limousine, no doubt writing

her apology speech. But Garrett was pretty sure breakfast would lure the woman out of the car. They hadn't had a decent meal since Salt Lake City.

"Three?" Linda frowned.

Garrett nodded.

Linda shrugged and headed back toward the kitchen. "I'll bring out more silverware then."

"How long will it be before you're ready?" Garrett called after her.

"Give us ten minutes." Linda swung open a door to the kitchen and walked into the other room.

Nicki decided disaster had been averted. She didn't know where Linda got such strange ideas, but hopefully Nicki had set the record straight. "Since we have to wait, I think I'll go over to the hardware store and see if the pastor is there."

"I'll go with you."

Nicki hesitated and then decided it was just as well that Garrett didn't stay at the café within reach of Linda's voice. "Good."

Garrett cleared his throat when he opened the door for Nicki to step out into the street. "So you don't date?"

Nicki stopped walking.

Garrett grinned.

"Yeah, I don't much, either," Garrett said as he continued walking.

Nicki hurried to catch up with him.

The morning's light gave a crispness to Dry Creek. A thin layer of white snow coated the road and all of the buildings. Smoke came out of the large building across the street from the café. A dozen or so houses were scattered around the small business buildings. A church with a white steeple was set back off the main road to the east and a barn was set off the main road to the west.

It only took a few minutes to walk over to the hardware store.

Nicki could smell the burning wood as she stomped the snow off her boots on the porch outside the store. Pastor Matthew Curtis was clerking here, and he and his new wife, Glory, kept the potbellied stove in the middle of the large room going all day long when it was snowing. Several straight-backed wooden chairs were usually gathered around the stove and as often as not, a game of checkers was being played beside the stove. Glory kept her art easel set up by the window and painted portraits.

"I don't suppose they sell any jeans here?" Garrett asked as he put his hand around the stone-cold doorknob. He might as well be comfortable for the flight back to Vegas. If Lillian was staying, her chauffeur could come drive her back. That meant Garrett would need to fly back and he sure wasn't getting on any airplane dressed like a butler.

The hardware store door had a half-dozen small

panes of glass in it, but Garrett could not see inside the store because of the frost on the glass. He could already smell the flavored coffee brewing inside, though.

"They have overalls." Nicki couldn't picture Garrett wearing them. "Farmer overalls."

Garrett opened the door wide and then waited for Nicki to enter first.

Nicki had known the two old men sitting beside the stove all her life. In fact, Jacob Holmes's wife, Betty, had been her mother's best friend. After Betty died, Jacob spent his mornings at the hardware store.

They both looked up at her with smiles that turned to surprise when they saw Garrett come in behind her.

"Hi. Is Pastor Matthew around?" Nicki asked.

"The pastor?" Jacob was the first of the two men to recover his voice and his manners. He stood up and nodded to Garrett. "Pleased to meet you, young man. Any friend of Nicki's here is a friend of mine." Then Jacob turned to Nicki and beamed. "Of course, I can see he's more than a friend. We heard you had a fella heading out your way. And here I see he's already in his wedding suit and asking for the pastor. Are you eloping or something?"

Nicki froze. Here was where the thunderbolt reached down from the sky and struck her. Please, let it strike her. "Garrett's not—"

"We don't need the pastor." Garrett frowned and then realized what all the whispering had been about. "I know it looks like I'm in a tuxedo, but it's really just a chauffeur's uniform."

"Looks like a tuxedo to me," Jacob said suspiciously. "You're not just trying to pull the wool over our eyes are you, young man, so you can marry our Nicki with no one knowing?"

The sudden vision of what it would be like to be married to Nicki made his knees shake as if he were heading downhill in Big Blue with no brakes. But his throat didn't close up like he'd have expected. At least he could still breathe. He wondered why that was.

"Garrett is a stranger. He's just passing through. We don't know each other. And we are not dating."

Garrett frowned. She could have been a little less emphatic—just to be polite. She swatted the whole idea away as if it was annoying. Maybe that's why his allergic reaction didn't kick in. Nicki was making it clear she had no interest in even dating him, let alone marrying him. Which should make him feel good. "We're not strangers. You know my name."

Jacob nodded and turned to Garrett. "You wouldn't be the first man to be smitten with a Redfern woman before he knew more than her name. Nicki here is a prize. I knew her father—shoot, I knew her grandfather before that. I used to work on the Redfern Ranch back in the good old days when it was the biggest ranch between Canada and Texas. I wouldn't take kindly to some man doing wrong by her.''

''He's not—'' Nicki wondered how many ways a person could die from embarrassment. ''He's not doing me wrong. He's not doing anything. He's not smitten with me.''

Did Jacob ever look at her? Nicki wondered. She wasn't exactly a femme fatale in her barn-cleaning clothes.

Jacob kept his eyes narrowed on Garrett. ''It's a funny thing about the Redfern women and love. Why, I remember hearing that your great-great-grandmother—''

Nicki knew she needed to stop this one. ''She wasn't a Redfern. She was an Enger. And she didn't agree to marry Matthew Redfern because she was in love with him, she just needed that gold nugget he was offering up in the saloon so she could take care of those little kids of hers.''

''Maybe so,'' Jacob agreed. ''But that doesn't explain what happened with your great-grandmother. Why she—''

''My great-grandfather didn't fall in love with her at first sight, either. He just told that to the ranch hands so they'd stop trying to win her in those poker games and get back to herding the cattle.''

"Well, still." Jacob didn't back down. "You've got the same blood running in your veins. The Redfern women always were a passionate lot." Jacob scowled at Garrett. "Not that you need to be knowing about that, young man."

Garrett grinned. "Yes, sir."

Nicki groaned. The thunderbolt was sounding better all the time.

No thunderbolt roared, but the phone did ring.

"Dang it, that phone's been ringing all morning," Jacob complained as he went to sit back down on his chair by the stove. "A man can't get any peace anymore."

"Well, why don't you answer it?" Nicki said as she walked over to the counter.

"It's not my phone," Jacob said righteously. He pulled his chair closer to the stove. "It's not polite to answer someone else's phone. Gotta be for the pastor. But he's been gone. Should be back soon but—"

"Hello," Nicki said into the phone.

"Is this Dry Creek?" a woman's voice asked. She sounded breathless, as if the woman was rushing and worried.

"Yes, can I help you?"

"This is the only Dry Creek number the operator had. I'm trying to locate a Mr. Redfern."

Reno? "I'm Mr. Redfern's sister."

"Oh. Is Lillian Fern there?"

"I can get her for you."

The woman gasped, as if she had seen something she didn't like. "There's no time for that. Just tell her I'm getting gas outside of Vegas and she's to stay where she is until I get there. This is Chrissy."

"Garrett's cousin?" Nicki asked, but the line was dead. The woman had hung up.

"That's Chrissy?" Garrett walked over to the counter. Why would Chrissy be calling the hardware store?

"She said my mot—I mean, Lillian is to stay here until she gets here. Chrissy's left Vegas."

"Chrissy's coming?" Garrett wondered if his cousin had had a change of heart and had decided not to get married after all. "Did she mention any fiancée?"

"No."

"So she's coming alone?"

Nicki shrugged. "Sounds like it."

Well, that's good news, Garrett thought. If Chrissy was just leaving Vegas, she'd be here sometime tomorrow morning. Maybe she'd be willing to stay with Lillian a few days and drive the older woman's limousine back to Vegas so he could fly back. "So she's coming here."

Jacob held his hands out to the heat that was coming from the potbellied stove. "Won't that be nice.

We could use some more young women in this town—especially if we're going to be having another wedding. Someone to help throw all that rice.''

"They use birdseed these days," the other old man, Elmer, said as he looked up from the wooden stove. He had his shoes off and his legs stretched out toward the stove. "It's the modern way."

"But Nicki's an old-fashioned girl. She'll want rice." Jacob had a satisfied look on his face.

Nicki groaned. "No one's getting married."

"Well, you never know, now, do you?" Jacob drawled as he tipped back his chair. "We've had us a whole lot of weddings ever since last Christmas when the angel came to town."

"She wasn't a real angel," Nicki hastened to add. She didn't want Garrett to think they were completely nuts. "She just played the angel in the Christmas pageant."

"You should have heard her sing," Jacob reminisced. "Almost made me cry. It's a wonder Santa Claus had the heart to shoot at her afterward."

Nicki groaned. "It was a hit man that had dressed up as Santa Claus who tried to kill her."

"I see," Garrett said, appearing bewildered.

"Of course, the reverend risked a bullet to save the angel," Jacob continued.

"That's because he was in love with her," Nicki finished the story for the old man. Everyone knew how the story ended. "Well…and the twins—that would be his young sons—would have been broken-hearted if something had happened to their angel."

No wonder she was having those fairy-tale dreams, Nicki thought to herself. After all of the excitement and romance in Dry Creek lately, it was a miracle she wasn't flying off to enter some dating show in Hollywood. "But all of that romance is behind us now. Matthew and Glory are just another married couple. Dry Creek really is a very quiet little town."

"I see."

Nicki groaned. There was no way a stranger would see that Dry Creek really was a nice sensible place. At least no one had mentioned the rustlers that had kidnapped a local rancher and his girlfriend—well, she wasn't his girlfriend at the time, but she soon came to be. There seemed to be something about danger that made people fall in love around here.

"You know the pastor is going to insist on doing marriage counseling with the two of you," Elmer said thoughtfully as he leaned forward from his chair and cupped his hands around the warmth coming from the woodstove.

"We don't have any need for—" Nicki groaned at the disapproving look on Elmer's face.

"Now, I know you try to hide it, but you've had bad feelings about church ever since your mother left. And I can't fault you for that, but that don't mean you can just wave God goodbye on the most important day of your life.''

''I'm not waving God goodbye. I'm not having an important day.''

Elmer grunted in disapproval and turned his eyes to Garrett. ''And you, young man—are you planning to ditch marriage counseling, too?''

Garrett had forgotten that pastors knew more about marriages than anyone else. They certainly attended more weddings than the average person. Maybe that's where he could get some advice on what to say to Chrissy just in case she hadn't jilted her boyfriend. ''Not on your life. If someone claims to have the answers to getting married, I'll sit down and listen.''

Elmer beamed. ''That's the attitude. The pastor will be glad to know you're open to talking. Now that he's married again, he sure does like to see people walk down the aisle.''

Nicki knew her face was getting red. She didn't want to open her mouth because she knew she would sputter. Elmer was the kind of man whose mind ran on a single track. He wasn't going to let go of his marriage idea unless something came along and knocked that idea off his track.

''Lester's been stopping by the ranch, you know.''

''Lester Wilkerson?'' Elmer frowned. ''I know he picks up your mail and has been asking around about what kind of feed you buy for your cattle, but I wouldn't think he'd be the one for you.''

''Well, he's asked me out.''

''Didn't he bring you and your brother to the Christmas pageant?'' Jacob asked with a matching frown.

''He likes to include the family. Family is important to him.''

Elmer shook his head. ''If he ain't out-and-out asked, you've got no obligation to wait for him. But it does make me think you'd do good to hear what the pastor has to say about getting married.''

''I am not getting married,'' Nicki said through clenched teeth. ''What I am going to do is go back over to the café and have breakfast.''

Jacob nodded sagely as he leaned back in his chair. ''I read in *Woman's World* that people in love eat more. Of course, it's mostly chocolate.''

That stopped Nicki. Jacob had ridden the range with her father. ''What are you doing reading *Woman's World*?''

Jacob tilted his head toward the small table that stood behind the stove. ''Glory says we need to keep informed so she brings in her magazines. That's where Elmer read about the birdseed at weddings.''

Elmer frowned. ''I didn't know there was so much to know about getting married. It'd make a man think twice about it all if he knew what was involved in guest lists and place cards.''

''Well, fortunately, we're not getting married,'' Garrett said as he started to make his move for the door. Of course, he couldn't go without taking Nicki with him and she was looking shell-shocked.

''We just met,'' Nicki added for emphasis. ''We're just both hungry. We're not even dating.''

Garrett stopped. He was forgetting something. ''You say those magazines tell you how to do a wedding? With all the trimmings?''

Elmer nodded. ''Step by step.''

''Save them for me, will you?'' Just in case Chrissy didn't stop her wedding, maybe she'd at least do it right and invite Aunt Rose.

Jacob beamed. ''You can pick them up when you get back from your breakfast date.''

''Date?'' Nicki asked.

Elmer nodded. ''*Woman's World* would say it was. Eight out of ten readers said a meal alone together counts as a date.''

''Then it's not a date,'' Nicki stated firmly. ''My mother's going to be there.''

Nicki regretted mentioning her mother the minute she saw the shocked look on the faces of the two older men.

''Lillian's back?'' Jacob whispered. His face had turned white.

Nicki nodded miserably as she turned to go. "But she isn't staying."

"She's back?" Jacob said again to no one in particular.

"Yes," Nicki said softly as she started walking toward the door. How could she have forgotten? Jacob used to be her father's best friend just as Betty had been her mother's best friend. Jacob and Betty had been as upset with Lillian as her father had been.

Nicki remembered how withdrawn her father had been after Lillian left. For months, Nicki's father didn't want to see anyone, not even Jacob. Jacob would drive out to the ranch and Nicki's father would send him away. Finally, Jacob stopped coming. The only time the two men had seen each other since then was for Betty's funeral.

Jacob must blame Lillian for the loss of his best friend. He might even blame her for the sadness that Betty had until the day she died.

It seemed that Nicki wasn't the only one who would be upset by seeing Lillian Redfern again.

Nicki and Garrett stopped at the limousine before they walked back to the café, but Lillian waved them on. She had more to worry about than breakfast.

Lillian sat in the back of her limo with the envelope in front of her. No matter how many times she read the papers inside, the diagnosis remained the same. Cancer.

Oh, how she wished Charles were still here so she could talk to him. He'd always been the brave one when it came to facing problems. Her style was to run away. Even coming back to Dry Creek she needed to be sure no one pitied her. The limo was to prove she was somebody now.

Of course the cancer didn't care who she was.

And, before she went in for treatment, she had wanted to make things right with Charles.

Since Charles wasn't here, she'd just have to make things right with the whole town of Dry Creek instead.

Lillian just wished she didn't have to tell Nicki. She couldn't bear to hurt her little girl any more than she'd already been hurt by life. That's why she wouldn't have come back if she had known Nicki was here.

Chapter Six

Nicki swore she was going to walk home and sit in her kitchen where there was no prince, no limo and no mother. This day was so mixed-up, she was beginning to think she needed to start it over. After hearing Elmer and Jacob talk about reading *Woman's World,* nothing should have surprised her.

Nicki only had to open the door to the café to know the day had one more surprise for her. Everything was turned upside down inside the café too. Someone had strewn shiny red paper hearts all over the tables and floors. It looked as if there was something tacked to the walls, but she couldn't see what it was because the lights had been turned off and the window shades drawn down.

Without the morning light, the café was dim. It

would be deep dark except for the individual candles burning at each of the tables and on the high shelves that lined the room. The yellow light coming from the candles made the black-and-white floor of the café gleam.

Nicki sniffed. Gone was the smell of baking biscuits. In its place was the scent of raspberries and vanilla from the candles.

"Linda?" Nicki called out.

There was a love song coming from the radio in the kitchen that was so upbeat it would make a man on crutches want to start dancing.

Nicki looked up at Garrett. The candlelight touched his face and made him look like someone in a Renaissance painting. "I'm sorry, people aren't usually this—" Nicki looked around again "—strange."

Garrett smiled. "I have a feeling they're just campaigning for you to date someone other than this Lester fellow." Garrett decided he rather liked the people of Dry Creek. He'd always heard that people in small towns minded each other's business, and it looked as if Dry Creek was no exception. Maybe it wouldn't be so bad to have a whole town filled with dozens of Aunt Roses. Of course, they had *Woman's World* in addition to Aunt Rose. "I'll bet they have something all planned out from one of those magazines. Besides, they're having fun."

Garrett pulled out a chair for Nicki and she sank down into it as though she would really prefer to slide all of the way under the table. "The people in this town need to get a hobby."

"Sounds to me like they have one." Garrett decided the cold air had finally numbed his brain. He didn't even mind that half of the town's population was trying to set him up with the woman in front of him. If he couldn't outromance Lester, he'd have to retire from dating.

Garrett had to stop and remind himself he had stopped dating, at least for a while. He hoped that wasn't a bad omen.

"So what do people do around here for fun?" Garrett asked Nicki as he sat down in a chair opposite her. He wasn't going to give this one up without a fight.

"Besides torturing me?"

Garrett looked over at Nicki. Her cheekbones were high and there wasn't a trace of blush on them. But she sparkled in the candlelight from the melting snowflakes that had fallen on her as she'd walked back to the café.

"Well, there really is only one way to stop them," Garrett said. He waited until Nicki looked at him hopefully. She had the most amazing green eyes. Even in the candlelight, they changed color constantly. A man could get lost just looking into them.

"Yes?" Nicki finally prodded.

"Oh." Garrett cleared his throat. "We have to go on a date, that's all."

"A date?" Nicki squeaked.

Garrett nodded. "And not just any date. A date that would be better than anything *Woman's World* could offer."

Nicki was speechless. "You think they got this from the magazine?"

Garrett nodded and then suddenly remembered something. "And before you ask, your brother can't come."

"I wasn't—"

"And neither can this Lester fellow. Actually, especially not this Lester fellow. Let him get his own date."

Nicki was speechless, which was just as well because she heard Linda walking out from the kitchen.

"All set to order?" Linda held a small pad of paper in one hand and a pen in the other. Linda had changed her clothes so that she was wearing a chef's hat with a red ribbon tied around it and a long white formal dress with shiny red heart pockets. "The special of the day is heart pancakes with strawberries on top. It comes with scrambled eggs, bacon and hazelnut coffee."

"I've had breakfast here before—" Nicki said bewildered. "You never—" She waved her hand to indicate everything. "Even the dress."

"Left over from Halloween," Linda explained cheerfully. "I was the Queen of Hearts and Jazz was the Joker. We were reading one of Glory's *Woman's World* magazines, and it said people were more likely to eat out if it was a fun experience. So we thought costumes are fun. I wanted something that said good health—you know with the heart and all."

"So it's for health," Nicki said. "And *Woman's World*."

She looked over at Garrett. He winked at her.

Linda continued. "Well, eight out of ten women rank dining out as their favorite date. Jazz and I have maxed out the lunch crowd. If we want to expand, we need to have another angle. So we thought we'd turn to romance eating—you know, people eat more when they are in love."

"We heard."

"I'd eat here," Garrett offered. "It's a good idea to expand your menu."

"But they used to have regular pancakes." Nicki mourned. The whole world was going crazy around her.

"Nothing wrong with making them into hearts." Garrett defended the café.

Linda looked at Garrett and smiled. "I'm glad you feel that way. I talked to Jazz, and we decided you're the one we are looking for. I didn't think so at first, but you're a good choice. You could teach the men of Dry Creek a thing or two about romance. You've got the tuxedo and the look.''

''Me? This isn't a tuxedo. It's a chauffeur's uniform. And it's not even mine. I'm a trucker. I don't have a look. I'm not a romantic kind of guy. I hate poetry. Can't stand the opera.''

Linda walked over to a shelf and pulled down a magazine, flipping it open. ''Would you buy a woman roses in the middle of winter?''

''Well, yes.''

Linda eyed him as she looked over the magazine. ''Not just something planted in a pot, but the real thing—those long-stemmed ones.''

''Yeah.''

Nicki remembered the orchid blossom that Lester had gotten for her. ''Roses don't last long in winter.'' She almost sighed, but she felt she owed it to Lester to defend him. ''They're not a practical choice.''

Linda waved Nicki's objection aside and kept questioning Garrett. ''Question number five. If you were out on a date and a robber threatened to shoot your date unless she gave him her purse, what would you do?''

''Tell her to give it to him.''

Linda kept reading in the magazine. ''What if she refused and the man held up his gun?''

"Can I knock the gun out of his hand?"

Linda looked up from the magazine. "No."

"Well, where are the police?"

"Not close by. And the robber is counting to three. He's already said two. What do you do?"

"I step in front of her—"

"Excellent choice."

"—and rip the purse out of her hands and give it to the man."

"Oh." Linda looked down the column. "You would be a hero for stepping in front of her, but it doesn't say anything about taking her purse away from her. I think you lose points for that."

"I'm not going to die for some woman's lipstick."

"Not all women want some man to be their hero, either," Nicki said firmly. Where did Linda get this nonsense? "It's better to let the authorities deal with things."

"I asked about the police," Garrett protested.

"That's good. That's the right thing to do." Nicki was getting a headache. "It doesn't matter what the magazine says, people need to use common sense."

"Common sense never made anyone fall in love," Linda said softly as she pulled her order pad out of her hand again. "So, what will it be, folks?"

Nicki hadn't meant to hurt Linda's feelings. A woman Linda's age was supposed to be giddy about love. Nicki gave up. "I believe I'll have the heart special."

"Really?" Linda brightened. "With the strawberries?"

"With extra strawberries if you have them."

"Make that two specials," Garrett added with a grin. "And I swear I'll take a bullet if someone tries to steal it away from me."

"You're only supposed to take the bullet if they try to steal Nicki's," Linda said softly. "It doesn't count if you're protecting your own breakfast."

"In that case, I'll have a side of bacon with that." Nicki smiled. "Now that I know it's safe."

Nicki should give a man some warning when she was going to smile like that, Garrett thought. His mouth went dry from the beauty of seeing it. Her green eyes lit up like jewels and sparkled with fun.

"You're beautiful." Garrett wasn't aware that he had spoken aloud until he saw the surprised look on Nicki's face. "I mean, it's beautiful—the café and all."

"Oh, yes." Nicki seemed relieved.

"We need some publicity on this one though," Linda said as she tapped her pen to her order pad. "You know, something that will get the romantic idea across—we can't just advertise heart-shaped pancakes. It needs to be more to make the married folks come out on a cold winter morning and have breakfast together. We've thought of making a poster.''

''You don't need a poster. Just take a picture of your breakfast and tack it up on the bulletin board over at the hardware store. All of the men around here go into the hardware store at least once a week. They'd see it.''

''Great idea—Jazz has a camera in back, we could take some pictures right now if it's all right with the two of you.''

Why did Garrett have the feeling he and Nicki had been led down this path a little too smoothly? Oh, well, let the kids have their fun.

Garrett looked at Nicki. ''I don't mind if they snap a picture or two of our plates before they bring them out of the kitchen, do you?''

''Oh, the plates won't be enough,'' Linda reached over and moved the candle on the table so that it reflected off Garrett's face even more. ''To sell romance. We need romance. We need you two in the pictures.''

''Us?'' Nicki said, then she blurted out what she really meant. ''Garrett's great. He's dressed for it. Can't you just use his picture?''

''One man sitting alone and eating heart-shaped pancakes? That's not romantic. In fact, it's kind of creepy.'' Linda looked more closely at what Nicki was wearing. ''Oh.''

"I should have worn a dress."

"Don't worry. I have just the thing." Linda started walking toward the back of the kitchen. "The Queen of Hearts costume came with a whole bunch of other costumes. They're made out of paper, but that won't show in the picture. One or two will even go with the tuxedo."

"Uniform," Garrett corrected automatically.

Nicki looked over at Garrett. She had to give the man credit. He seemed to be enjoying himself. She couldn't help but think that Lester would have stormed out of the café by now. Maybe that's why he never talked about anything but the weather. Maybe he didn't allow himself to do enough things in life.

"I've never been in a commercial before—" Garrett wondered how he could get the conversation back to where they'd left off. A photo of romance was fine, but he wanted a date with Nicki before people forgot about *Woman's World* and he lost his excuse. "I wonder what else people do around here to date."

"People in Dry Creek don't date." Nicki frowned slightly. "I know it sounds like they do because of the way everyone's been trying to get you to take me out on a date. But don't worry. There's no place to go on a date anyway. You're safe."

Garrett was beginning to suspect Nicki didn't want

to go out on a date with him. "There must be some-place people go."

"Well, there is the café, but we're already here." Nicki wondered if she should suggest that Garrett frown while the picture was being taken. In his tux-edo, the frown made him look fierce. Which was pretty much how most of the men in town would feel about taking their wives out to a romantic breakfast. He might pull in some viewer empathy that way. "The kids go over to the mountains in the summer evenings and party some."

Garrett caught his breath in his throat. "You'd go there with me?"

"It's winter. Nobody goes there in the winter. It's cold."

"Well, where do people go in the evenings around here?"

Nicki shrugged. "Tonight they're having a Thanksgiving Eve service at church."

Garrett heard the sound of boots on the porch out-side the café. He didn't want to get interrupted again. "Let's go there, then."

Church certainly wasn't equal to a moonlight eve-ning in the summer, but Garrett wasn't going to quib-ble at this point in time. He'd told himself he'd have a date with Nicki, and he wasn't going to shy away just because he'd never even heard of a church date before—in fact, he couldn't remember the last time he'd been inside a church. "What's a Thanksgiving Eve service?"

"Everyone brings a candle and they light it and tell something they are thankful for—"

The door to the café opened.

"What happened to the lights?" Elmer asked as he stepped inside. "Something wrong with the electricity?"

"Nothing's wrong with the electricity at the church. And we're on the same line." Another man stepped into the café.

"Pastor Matthew?" Nicki asked as she looked up.

The door from the kitchen opened again, and Linda came back out with several long dresses draped over her arm. "I've got the costumes. Take your pick. Jazz is looking for the camera."

"We're making an advertisement," Nicki explained to the three men who were now inside the café. Jacob had been the last to enter. "Something to make men bring their wives in for a romantic breakfast."

Elmer grunted suspiciously. "Isn't bacon and eggs enough to bring in the customers?"

"Not according to *Woman's World*," Garrett explained.

"Oh." Elmer nodded.

Linda stopped at the table where Nicki and Garrett sat. She held up the first of the paper dresses. It had a red cross on it in several places and a paper stethoscope in the pocket. "No, that won't do. Jazz wouldn't like to have a nurse in the picture. It'd give people a bad feeling about the café."

The next costume was of a judge. Linda tossed it aside. "Not very romantic."

"But orderly." Nicki wasn't so fast to give up on the judge costume. "And it matches Garrett's tuxedo—I mean the uniform—and it's dignified."

"Dignified's not romantic."

"But it's nice."

"No, this is what we need." Linda held up the last costume.

"Oh," Nicki breathed out.

Nicki heard four men echo her.

It was a princess costume.

"That pink reminds me of the inside of a seashell I saw once when I was a boy," Elmer said. "I've never forgotten it."

The skirt on the dress flared out and had dozens of tiny tucks drawn onto it. The bodice plunged low and the cleavage that was drawn on the paper would have made any prince drool. "I can't wear that. It's—"

"It's winter out, that's why." Garrett hoped they didn't choose the princess outfit. It made his breath stop just to look at the dress and then to think of Nicki wearing it. He certainly didn't want to be sitting in church with those thoughts in his head. He'd be excommunicated for sure, and he hadn't even joined anything.

"Well, we'll take the pictures inside, of course," Linda told him.

"Of course."

"Just as soon as Nicki puts the dress on, in fact."

A bell rang in the kitchen and Linda turned. "Your specials are ready. I'll be right back with them. Nicki, you can just pull that dress over what you're wearing."

"I smell bacon," Elmer said as he pulled a chair over to the table beside Garrett and Nicki. "Mind if I join you?"

"Me, too," Jacob said as he found another chair. "That smells mighty fine."

"Well, I only came over because they said you were looking for me," Pastor Matthew said, but he pulled over a chair all the same.

Garrett was beginning to see why no one dated in Dry Creek. They were never alone long enough.

"It was my mother who wanted to see you," Nicki told the pastor as she stood up. "Maybe she'd like to talk to you in the limousine. There's more privacy there."

Nicki hoped her mother would talk to Pastor Matthew in the limousine. That way her mother could ease her conscience and not be so public about it all.

"I'm going to go in the kitchen and put on my dress."

"But it's paper. Stay away from the grill." Garrett saw another reason why people didn't date in Dry Creek. You felt responsible for a person before you even had the opportunity to date them. It wasn't quite fair. It made it hard for a man to concentrate on his moves. "I'd better come with you."

"To put on her dress?" Elmer said as he started to rise.

"It's just a costume," Garrett protested. "It'll go over all her other clothes."

"Oh." Elmer sat down.

Garrett felt all three men watch him as he followed Nicki into the kitchen. Then again, this might be the main reason nobody dated in Dry Creek. There were too many chaperones.

Garrett couldn't remember ever dating anyone who was so protected. He'd have thought it would bother him, but it didn't. He liked knowing there were men who would take care of Nicki and protect her from someone like him. It was depressing to know that he was the kind of man that a town wouldn't want their favorite daughter to date. But he couldn't fault the men for their judgment. They knew he wasn't the kind of man who stayed around for long.

Still, he wished he was sitting back out there with those three men and scowling at the back of some other stranger passing through instead of being the stranger himself.

Chapter Seven

Garrett changed his mind. He didn't wish he was anywhere else in the world right now except inside the kitchen of Dry Creek's café.

The men outside in the dining area didn't know it, but they should have followed him into the kitchen. Garrett was standing so close to Nicki he could feel every curve along her back. He blessed the makers of those paper dresses, whoever they were.

The paper dress didn't just slip on easily. It had to be coaxed over the sweater Nicki was wearing, inch by blessed inch.

Garrett had not noticed the back of Nicki's neck until now. She had reached up and clipped her hair behind her so it didn't get in the way of pulling the dress on. Garrett had already brushed his hand across her hair several times and, if he was lucky, he'd feel its wispy softness several more times before they left the kitchen.

"It's stuck," Nicki said.

Garrett could feel her nervousness and frustration in the way she held her back. "It's just got a twist here."

Garrett reached up and smoothed the hair off of Nicki's neck before he let his hand smooth the paper dress over her shoulder. "We're almost done."

Nicki grunted. "We'd better be."

No one was in the kitchen but the two of them. Linda and Jazz were outside in the other part of the café arranging their breakfast plates.

Garrett gave the dress one last tug. "There."

The dress covered Nicki from her neck to her toes. Even her arms were covered. Still, the whole thing made her feel naked.

"A princess wouldn't really wear something like this, would she?" Nicki looked down at the dress. The drawing showed as much paper skin as it did paper dress. Nicki had tucked the collar and sleeves of her sweater inside the costume so it was just her head sticking out. "It would shock the palace."

While Nicki talked, she had slowly turned around until she was facing Garrett. The morning light filled the kitchen and the air smelled like biscuits and bacon.

Garrett was speechless. No wonder all the princesses he'd ever heard about had become queens. If women dressed like that today, they'd get all the political votes, at least the ones from the men.

"I can't walk in this," Nicki said as she started to move toward the door leading to the rest of the café. The paper dress trailed along with her. "You'll have to carry the train to this thing."

Nicki opened the door to the main room of the café.

Garrett was glad that Linda had covered the windows. Not that it looked as if there was anyone left to peek in the windows from the street outside. All of the people of Dry Creek must have come inside while he and Nicki were in the kitchen.

"Oh, there you are." Nicki's mother was standing at the front of the crowd. Jacob and Elmer were on one side and the young couple who ran the café stood on the other side. "I'm getting ready to say my few words."

"Now?" Nicki squeaked. There wasn't any place to hide. Maybe if she had Garrett lift the train on her dress a little higher she could crawl under it. She might look like a garden slug, but she'd be hidden.

Lillian Redfern looked around and frowned. "No, I can't speak yet. Mabel Hargrove isn't here. She'd never forgive me if she wasn't here when I said what I have to say."

"Good," Linda said as she motioned for Nicki and Garrett to come forward. "We have time to get the pictures taken first then. We don't want the food to be cold for the pictures."

"No one can tell if the food is cold," Nicki reassured her as she sat down.

The table was set for romance. A red napkin was laid carefully across the middle of the table, as if it was an afterthought. Three candles of different lengths stood beside the salt and pepper shakers. A plate of strawberries sat to the right of a small pitcher of cream. Water glistened on the just-washed strawberries.

Jazz, tall and thin, was standing and frowning at the table. "I don't want any shadows hanging over the table." He looked up at the people crowded around the table and lifted an eyebrow.

"I'll go out on the porch and wait," Pastor Matthew offered as he nudged one of the older men.

"And I'll go ask Mabel Hargrove to come over here," Elmer said as he reluctantly backed away from the table. "Just don't start anything without me."

"And, Lillian and I—" Jacob looked around for an excuse. "We'll go sit over in the corner. You won't even know we're here."

Jazz had the camera to his eye before anyone even stepped away from the table. "Let's try this angle first.'' He brought the camera away from his eye and frowned. ''No, that's not right. Maybe if we try it from some height.''

It took Jazz ten minutes to decide the angle of his first shot. Garrett was sitting at the table and his jaw was beginning to ache from smiling so much.

''I can't hold this much longer,'' Nicki said through clenched teeth. She sat at the table across from Garrett. Her hand was falling asleep as she held her spoon in midair. ''No one eats eggs with a spoon anyway.''

''Creative license.'' Linda was in charge of the staging. She shifted the spoon slightly so it got more candlelight. ''Have you ever noticed the way a spoon reflects the light? It's so much more elegant than a fork. Once we start shooting it won't take long.''

Linda pulled away from the table and Jazz snapped the picture.

''Look dreamy now,'' Linda said as Jazz repositioned himself.

''Dreamy?'' Nicki wondered if cross-eyed would do.

Linda nodded. ''Like you're in love. Remember, romance sells pancakes here.''

Nicki had avoided looking at Garrett for that very reason. She didn't want her heart to be out there for anyone who was interested in buying a pancake to see.

Jazz took four more shots before he mentioned the strawberries. "For the last one, let's do a strawberry shot."

"I'm starving." Nicki thought it might be worth mentioning.

"And she almost fainted once this morning," Garrett added helpfully.

"The food's getting cold." Nicki nodded.

"We'll heat it up for you." Linda sprinkled some pepper on the eggs. "Besides, you'll like the next shot. It involves food."

"We get to eat the eggs?"

Linda shook her head until her earrings swayed. She picked up a whole strawberry from the plate. "You get to split this."

Half of a strawberry didn't look like enough to halt her hunger pangs, but Nicki lifted her knife anyway. She'd be fair.

"No, you don't split it with your knife. You kiss it apart."

"What?"

Garrett was starting to grin. He had a feeling he was going to see more of those green sparks fly out of Nicki's eyes.

"With our lips?" Nicki looked skeptical. "Can't we just each take a bite? That's a lot more sterile."

Linda shook her head and held the strawberry out

to Nicki. "Just hold it in your teeth. Garrett will do the rest."

"I—" Nicki was silenced with a strawberry.

Garrett had barely begun to kiss Nicki when Jazz took the first picture.

Nicki wondered why she'd never really tasted a strawberry before. The fruit was warm and soft and sweet with just a hint of something stronger. Maybe the strong part was Garrett's lips. No, they were the soft part.

Jacob had to clear his throat three times before Nicki realized the flashing had stopped.

"Oh." Nicki pulled away from Garrett. She wondered if she had the same bewildered look on her face that he had on his. "Something was wrong with that strawberry. You must have soaked it in something."

Linda grinned. "You liked it, huh?"

Nicki didn't have to answer because the door to the café opened and Mrs. Hargrove walked in.

"Where is she?" Mrs. Hargrove hadn't bothered to put on her coat or take the metal curlers out of her hair. She was wearing a green-checked gingham dress with a white apron over it and clutching a coin purse in her hand. She entered the café and looked in all directions until her gaze settled on Lillian. "There you are."

Nicki felt the blood start to flow in her veins again.

It was time someone gave her mother a good scolding and Mrs. Hargrove was just the person to do it. Mrs. Hargrove had taught the first grade Sunday school class for the past thirty years in Dry Creek and she didn't hesitate to speak her mind.

"Hello, Mabel," Nicki's mother said as she stood. "You're looking well."

"I've got baking powder on my face and curlers in my hair. I know I look a fright." Mrs. Hargrove studied Lillian where she stood. "You dyed your hair blond."

Lillian nodded. "I've worn it that way for years now."

"You could have written, you know. I worried about you."

"I didn't think you'd want to hear from me—not after I took the money."

Mrs. Hargrove shrugged. "Charles and Jacob paid it back."

"Oh." Lillian frowned. "I didn't mean for anyone to do that. I meant to sneak into some Sunday service and slip it into the offering plate. At first, anyway. Then I was worried someone would recognize me and I didn't know what I would say."

Mrs. Hargrove nodded. "I see how that could be."

"I want to pay it back now though." Lillian had a purse strap on her shoulder and she swung the purse around to open it. "I could write a check."

"You can't just write a check," Nicki protested. If Mrs. Hargrove wasn't going to scold her mother, someone else would have to do it. "Money can't make up for the hurt you caused the people around here."

"You're right. I did mean to apologize first and ask everyone to forgive me." Lillian looked at the people in the café. "Do you forgive me for doing something so foolish?"

Lillian smiled and blinked as if she were on the verge of tears.

Elmer caved first. "Don't mention it."

Mrs. Hargrove wasn't far behind. "We just worried about you, not the money."

Jacob looked at Lillian, but he didn't say anything.

"Nicki's right, though," Pastor Matthew said, and everyone looked to him. "Money isn't enough."

Lillian smiled. "I meant to include a little extra for the minister of the church, as well."

"I don't take bribes," Pastor Matthew said mildly. "I was just thinking that if you spent some time praying about it, you might think of a better way to make peace with the people of Dry Creek."

"Pray about it?" Lillian covered her surprise quickly. "Why, yes, of course, I can do that."

Nicki felt that someone was finally taking her mother's actions seriously. Good for the pastor.

"Maybe Nicki can pray with you about it," Pastor Matthew continued.

"Me?" Nicki decided the pastor was going too far.

"It'll do the two of you good to pray together," Elmer said.

"We'll all pray about it," Mrs. Hargrove said decisively. "That's what friends and family are for."

Garrett was liking the people of Dry Creek better the longer he was around them. They were an odd group of people, but he could see they were loyal to each other. Kind of like Aunt Rose would be if she was here.

"And, of course there's the Thanksgiving service tonight," Elmer suggested. "We'll all be there, won't we?"

Elmer looked around for nods.

"I'll be there. Nicki and I have a date," Garrett volunteered.

"Really." Pastor Matthew brightened. "You're coming to the Thanksgiving service on a date?"

Garrett nodded cautiously. He wondered if anyone else had ever used church as a dating plan in Dry Creek—he supposed not even Lester had sunk that low.

"I'll have to throw in a few of the love verses in my meditation," the pastor said. "You know the 'love is' ones."

Garrett nodded. He had no idea what the man was talking about.

"I always liked those." Mrs. Hargrove smiled. "'Love is patient. Love is kind.' They are true, true words."

"If you're going to be talking about love, maybe you could mention our pancake heart special," Jazz suggested. "You know just at some break or something."

"I could mention it in the announcements," the pastor said. "Sort of a community service thing."

"Good." Jazz put the cap back on his camera lens. "And tell people to look for the pictures in the hardware store of the guy in the tuxedo."

Garrett felt as if his smile was frozen on his face. He turned to Nicki. "You said the store sells some kind of overalls?"

"We'll go back after breakfast." She was just as anxious as he was to get him into other clothes. No man sparkled in farmer overalls. Once Garrett didn't have the tuxedo anymore, she was sure he'd settle down into looking really quite ordinary.

Nicki sure hoped so. Ever since the strawberry kiss she'd felt her appetite slowly leaving her. She'd never had even the smallest dent in her appetite around Lester. Maybe she was catching a cold or something.

"Do you have more of those strawberries?" Garrett asked Linda as he poured some syrup on his heart-shaped pancake. "They're some of the sweetest ones I've ever eaten."

Linda gave him a strange look. "They're frozen without sugar. Jazz said they were bitter. He wanted to return them to the supplier."

"I thought maybe they had something on them— maybe that's what Jazz thought was bitter." Nicki decided her eggs weren't too cold to eat and looked around for her fork. All she had was a spoon.

"What's in the eggs?" Nicki frowned. She guessed it tasted good, it just didn't taste like eggs.

"Jazz added some grated Parmesan cheese and a sprinkling of dill."

"Humm." Nicki took her second spoonful. They weren't bad. "They kind of set off the pancakes."

Nicki was beginning to see that married people in Dry Creek might like to have a special breakfast at the café. The breakfast would give them something to talk about at home. It might even change the way everyone cooked eggs. A change might be a good thing. How long had everyone in Dry Creek been cooking their eggs the same way anyway?

Chapter Eight

Nicki knew she was wrong about the eggs by the time she finished eating them. They sat in her stomach and protested. Maybe there was a reason everyone made their eggs the same way they always had.

She knew she was also wrong about Garrett's tuxedo the minute she saw him wearing the overalls he was planning to buy over at the hardware store. It hadn't been the tuxedo that sparkled. No, the tuxedo was draped over a chair in the stockroom where she couldn't even see it, and her mouth was going dry just looking at Garrett in the overalls. It was him that sparkled, not his clothes.

Of course, he wasn't making it easy for her.

"You'll freeze to death," Nicki informed him. "Nobody wears those overalls without a shirt."

Where did the man think he was anyway? Venice Beach?

Garrett could pose for the sexy farmer calendar if they had one that went with the sexy firemen and sexy policemen ones. She looked at him closer. What was a truck driver doing with a tan in November? And muscles?

Nicki had seen her share of haying crews, and the sight of working men with muscles was not new to her. She'd even seen those same men shirtless and her only thought had been that someone was saving on the laundry. She wondered if she had been missing something before. Maybe she just hadn't been paying attention or she was too worried about whatever crop was being harvested. Maybe that was it.

"Just give me a minute," Garrett said as he frowned and moved his shoulders. "I don't think this shirt is the right size, either."

Glory had stepped from behind the counter in the hardware store to get Garrett the clothes he wanted. She was walking up to him now with a black shirt in her hand. "Maybe this will fit."

Glory took the shirt and measured it against Garrett's back.

Nicki frowned. She supposed Garrett liked to have Glory smooth the shirt across his back like that. What man wouldn't? Glory was beautiful. She had coppered-red hair and skin that was all white and pink. The people of Dry Creek would always think of her as their angel because of the part she played in the Christmas pageant. Nicki thought she looked the part. Yes, any man would like to have someone like Glory fuss over him.

"Glory's married, you know," Nicki offered, just in case their was any question on the matter.

Garrett looked over at Nicki, puzzled. "I know. To the pastor, isn't it?"

Garrett smiled at Glory. "I really appreciate all the time you're taking with me. I would be lost without it."

Nicki frowned.

Glory smiled back. "It's not easy to find things in the store yet. We're working on organization, but we haven't gotten past the bolts. The twins were helping us with them and we got sidetracked."

"Glory's a mother now, too," Nicki added just in case Garrett didn't understand what the mention of the twins actually meant.

"And loving every minute of it," Glory agreed. "They keep me busy."

"I think this one'll fit," Garrett said as he took the black shirt from Glory's hands. "I'll just go in the back and put it on."

Glory watched Garrett step into the back room before she turned to Nicki. "He's a nice man. I'm so happy for you. Jacob and Elmer—" she nodded her head toward the potbellied stove even though the chairs around it were now empty "—they told me how it is."

"I told them a dozen times Garrett doesn't know me. He just drove my mother up here and he's hanging around until she's ready to leave. He'll be back in Vegas before the tuxedo is due back at the rental place."

Glory smiled. "If he's hanging around, that's something. I was only hanging around when I met Matthew, and look what happened."

"Yes, but Matthew—he wanted to get married."

Glory arched her eyebrow. "Not when we first met. He thought I was some kind of a freak because his little boys thought I was a real angel and he thought I told them I was."

"Yes, but it didn't take him long to change his mind when he saw how pretty you are."

Glory straightened a shovel as she walked back to the counter. "Well, you're pretty, too, so maybe Garrett will change his mind."

Nicki wondered if anyone in Dry Creek ever really looked at her or if they were just all being overly polite. "Well, I'm healthy. And I suppose my teeth are all right."

Glory stepped behind the counter and laughed. "Don't sell yourself short. It's not just your teeth. You could be a striking woman if you wanted to be."

"What do you mean?"

"You've got the bone structure and your eyes are dramatic with all those greens. A little touch of makeup here and there and you could have any man you wanted eating out of your hands."

Nicki sighed. "I've been thinking I should marry Lester. It's the practical thing to do."

"Not if you don't want to marry him." Glory stepped out from behind the counter again. "Let me show you what I mean about that makeup. I've got all my stuff over at the house, but if you watch the store here for a minute or two I'll go get it. It won't take but a few minutes. Everybody's still over at the café anyway so no one will probably even come by."

Glory was right. Nicki could see out the window of the hardware store and into the open door of the café. The café windows were all fogged up from the breathing of the dozen or so people inside. And the people weren't just breathing. Nicki could see them shaking with laughter. "Wonder what they're talking about."

"Matthew said your mother was telling them stories about her Vegas dance days. I'm surprised you're not there listening, too."

Nicki smiled tightly. "I don't think I'd find those days as funny as everyone else does."

Glory nodded and walked over to where Nicki was standing by the window. "You missed her."

"I did fine."

Glory looked out the window toward the café. "I wonder why she left."

"Things here just weren't pretty enough for her." Nicki swore she could hear her mother from across the street. Or maybe Nicki was just remembering her mother's soft pleasing laugh. Her mother had always liked fine things. "I suppose that's what she liked about Vegas. All those dancers in those pretty costumes." Nicki turned to Glory. "Have you ever been to Vegas?"

Glory nodded. "It's not all that pretty. I like Dry Creek a lot better."

Nicki shrugged. "I've never been there. I thought about it a time or two, but it always seemed too complicated. What if I saw her on the street someplace?"

"Well, I'm glad she came back to Dry Creek." Glory gave Nicki a hug. "She should get to know you."

"Oh, there won't be time enough for that." Nicki backed away a little. She didn't want all of Dry Creek to go sentimental on her. "I don't think she's staying long."

"Who's not staying long?" Garrett walked out of the back room with the black shirt all buttoned up.

"My mother."

Glory waved goodbye from the doorway before she left the store.

"I had thought we were just going to be here for a few hours. But now with Chrissy coming—" Garrett realized he wasn't in as much of a rush to get back on the road as he had been. "I know it's an imposition since tomorrow is Thanksgiving, but I'd like to stay another day if that's all right with you? Chrissy should be pulling in sometime tomorrow. Your mother will probably want to stay in the house, but I can stay in the limo tonight."

"It's too cold for that. Reno won't mind if you stay in his room."

Nicki hadn't thought about the sleeping arrangements. Reno truly wouldn't mind if someone slept in his room while he was away, but that meant her mother would have to sleep in her father's old room. Neither Nicki nor Reno had seen any reason to change the room after their father died and her father hadn't given it much thought when he was alive. The last person to hang a picture or pick out a rug had been her mother. It would be like stepping back in a time warp for her.

"If you're planning to have anyone over for Thanksgiving or anything we can be gone for a few hours."

"We're not celebrating Thanksgiving at the ranch this year."

Garrett smiled. "In that case, the turkey soup is

on me—if there's a store around here to buy a few cans."

"There's no point in driving into Miles City for that—"

"Well, I'd buy a pumpkin pie, too." Garrett walked over to the window and looked across the street. "Maybe two pies if Chrissy is here and your brother."

"Reno should be back early morning. I guess he'd want to sit down to eat with—our mother." Nicki wasn't sure Reno was any more ready to see their mother than she was, but he deserved the chance to find out for himself how he felt about it. Nicki hoped he stopped at a pay phone on his way back and called, though, so she could warn him about their guest.

"I should go home and dust." She knew it was hopeless to expect her mother to have any good feelings about the home she left, but Nicki wanted the old place to be at its best.

Garrett turned back from the window. "I think it's breaking up over there. I was hoping the pastor would come back so I could pay him for the clothes." He already felt more like himself. The overalls were a little stiff, but they would do.

Garrett heard the sound of footsteps on the porch before the door to the hardware store burst open and a half-dozen people stomped inside. He was glad to see that the pastor was one of them. "I need to pay you for these."

The pastor walked toward the counter. "Before I work up a bill, let's figure out a good time to talk. I understand Jacob and Elmer tried to sign you up for marriage counseling a little prematurely."

"We're not getting married." Nicki wanted to be sure there was no lingering misunderstanding on that point. "I'm not sure I'll ever get married."

"I thought you were interested in Lester," Elmer said as he walked over to the potbellied stove and sat down in one of the chairs. "I was almost going to start looking through *Woman's World* for wedding gift ideas."

Garrett wondered where on the long highway he'd be when Nicki settled down and tied the knot with her Lester.

"She's not marrying Lester." Garrett glared at Nicki for emphasis. He sure hoped she wasn't fool enough to marry that man. Not that it was any of his business. But it did seem a waste if she was. Besides, he just remembered—"He hasn't even asked."

"Well, not in so many words. But when he does I just might say yes." Nicki glared right back at Garrett.

"Good," the pastor said before either one of them could carry the argument further. "Then you're both interested in getting married—just not to each other.''

''You can't do marriage counseling with two people who are going to marry other people.'' Nicki looked over at the stove where Elmer now sat, looking innocent. ''Did he put you up to this?''

''Me?''

''Well, I don't see why it wouldn't work.'' Garrett decided the pastor was on to something. This way he could prove to Nicki that she should not marry Lester. ''I'm sure there are times when people go in for counseling and then decide not to marry each other.''

Garrett looked to the pastor for confirmation and the man nodded.

''So what's different with us? If we're not going to marry each other, then we just know that up front instead of later. But we still get to think about all the questions.''

''Besides,'' Elmer said from his chair, ''your mother is over talking to Mrs. Hargrove and then Jacob wants to talk to her. She won't be ready to go home for another hour. You might as well give the pastor some practice on his counseling technique.''

''Oh.'' Nicki hadn't thought of it that way. She supposed Matthew did need to practice once in a while. ''Well, sure. I don't see why not.''

''The two of you can sit over here,'' Elmer said

as he got up from his chair. "I need to be getting home to do some chores anyway."

"I didn't think you did chores anymore since you retired." Nicki eyed the chair warily. "Don't leave because of us."

"People should have some privacy when they have marriage counseling." Elmer started to walk toward the door.

"That's only when the counseling is real," Nicki said, but she was too late. Elmer had already opened the door.

"It's a good thing Lester isn't here." Garrett went over and sat in one of the chairs. He liked the way they were grouped around the open stove that had the fire smoldering inside. "He might think it's a little insulting that his bride doesn't care if she talks about their marriage in front of the whole town."

Nicki's eyes started to spark just like Garrett had intended. He held back his smile. He didn't know which warmed him more—the fire to his left or Nicki's eyes to his right.

"I'm only going to be talking about marriage in general."

"Good. That's where we start with the counseling anyway," the pastor said as he pulled one of the chairs close to the fire and motioned for Nicki to take the one empty chair. "We need to talk about what you want out of marriage."

Garrett was surprised. "Isn't that kind of obvious?"

The pastor smiled. "Not always. That's why I have a series of questions that I start the session with."

"Okay. Let's go." Garrett decided he was going to enjoy this. He'd sure like to know what reason Nicki had for even considering marriage to a man like Lester.

"Well, first I'm going to ask which of the following you think is the most important to you in marriage." The pastor looked up at Garrett and then Nicki. "Common activity interests, common financial values, common family values, or a common faith?"

Garrett was lost already unless you counted sex as an activity interest. He did have a six-figure savings account and he owned Big Blue outright, but he didn't know that that was fancy enough to be called a financial value. He just hadn't had a lot to spend his money on once he had paid off Big Blue.

"Well, what do you think?" the pastor asked.

"For me, it's the land," Nicki said in a rush. "I don't know if that is family or financial or what— but I need to marry someone who understands I always want to be part of the Redfern Ranch."

The pastor nodded. "And that's important to you because…?"

''The land will always be there,'' Nicki answered without thinking. ''It can never leave me.''

''Ahh, like your mother did?'' The pastor nodded again as he marked something down on the tablet he held in his hand. ''Commitment to stay. I'll put that as a family/faith value. I can see that would be especially important for you because of your mother.''

Nicki looked around the hardware store to make sure no one else was in the place but the three of them. These questions were a little too revealing for her taste. ''I got along fine without my mother.''

Garrett had always thought that it was the sight of a crying woman that made him most want to ride in and save a woman from whatever was paining her. But he was wrong. The sight of Nicki fiercely holding back any sign of tears was even worse.

''You've done great,'' Garrett agreed loyally. ''Just great.''

''And you? What's important to you?'' Nicki turned to him.

''I just want to be able to make her tears go away,'' Garrett answered without thinking, and knew he had spoken the truth. Maybe that was half of the reason he'd stopped dating. He wanted to be more than a date to a woman.

''So, you want to be your wife's hero.'' The pastor nodded and wrote something on the tablet just like it was the most ordinary thing in the world. "Again, I'd say that's family values."

"Some women can take care of themselves," Nicki offered. She sure hoped Garrett wasn't going to end up with some whiny woman who didn't even know how to tie her own shoelaces. "Some women don't need a hero."

"Well, I don't need to be a hero everyday. It's just that—when the time comes, I want my wife to look to me for help."

Nicki scowled. She supposed she couldn't argue with that. It's just she had never been the kind of woman Garrett wanted to marry. She relied on herself in life and that was about it. She didn't even tell her problems to Reno. "Isn't that called codependency?"

The pastor chuckled. "It's natural for a man to want to protect and help his wife. I'm sure Lester will want to help you with your problems when you're married."

"Lester?" Nicki couldn't imagine telling her problems to Lester. Maybe that's why they never had any conversation beyond farming concerns. Still, she didn't like the smug look she saw on Garrett's face. "Yeah, sure. He does even now."

Garrett grunted.

"So we have two family value answers," the pastor said as he consulted his notebook. "Not bad."

Garrett snorted. "They couldn't be further apart as answers."

"Oh." The pastor looked up from his notebook. "I didn't know we were trying to match the answers. I thought you were both marrying other people."

Garrett groaned. "That's right. Lester and—Bonnie."

"Bonnie? I've never heard you talk about any Bonnie." Nicki knew she was right to not trust that man. He waited until now to tell her there was a Bonnie.

"Well, I haven't met her yet. But if you've got a Lester in your future, I can have a Bonnie."

"So you do plan to marry someday?" the pastor asked quietly. He didn't even mark anything in his notebook. "I got the impression you weren't really considering it."

"Well, I'm not." Garrett crossed his arms. He'd made that decision years ago. He should stick with it.

"So what does this Bonnie look like?" Nicki decided it was only fair that she know more about Bonnie since Garrett knew all there was to know about Lester.

"How would I know?"

"Well, you must have some picture in your head."

"She wears black spandex." Garrett knew it wasn't much to go on, but a picture was starting to form in his mind. "And her eyes are green—yeah, a real feisty kind of green that flash when she's upset."

"That could be anybody." Nicki crossed her arms.

Garrett didn't even need to look at her to know her eyes were flashing just like his mind was remembering. That would never do. Nicki clearly wasn't describing him as her ideal mate so he shouldn't describe her. "And she likes to ride with me in Big Blue—my truck."

"Where would you go?" Nicki was beginning to wish Garrett was the kind of guy who could put down roots. Not that she had a future with him anyway on account of the black spandex stuff. Black spandex was what men said when they wanted a woman who was exciting in all of the ways that Nicki wasn't. Garrett would probably even meet his Bonnie when he went back to Las Vegas. The city had lots of spandex women who'd like to meet a hero and drive off in Big Blue.

"I just go where my deliveries take me. No place special." Garrett frowned. He hadn't realized until now that he didn't have a special place to go to. One city was pretty much the same as the next one. A man ought to have a place that he longed to reach for more reasons than that he could deliver whatever he was carrying.

"I see." The pastor was thoughtfully looking at Garrett. "I'd say you don't like to be tied down. I hope—ah, Bonnie, is it?—feels the same way. Most women like to have a home.''

''I have a home. In the back of Big Blue's cab—there's a bed and a battery-operated television. I even have a small refrigerator.'' Garrett wondered when his life had gotten so depressingly single. ''The bed sleeps two if they're cozy.''

Nicki didn't like thinking of Bonnie in Garrett's bed. She turned her attention back to the pastor. ''Do you have any questions about how much conversation a married couple need to have for a good marriage?''

''Well, there's no set amount. But don't worry. You two seem to be talking pretty good.''

''I mean with Lester.''

''Oh.'' The pastor didn't even look down at his questions this time. ''I'd say if you're bothered by the amount of conversation, then there's a problem.''

''But if I'm not bothered, then it's okay?'' This was the first good news Nicki had heard in this whole time. She was fine with not talking to Lester.

''Well, I wouldn't exactly say that—''

The door opened and a gust of cold air blew into the store followed quickly by Glory. ''Sorry it took me so long.''

The pastor stood. ''That's all right. We were just doing a practice marriage counseling session.''

"Oh." Glory raised her eyebrow. "What makes it a practice one?"

"We're marrying different people." Nicki wondered how a woman ever got the kind of polish that Glory had. Her copper-colored hair waved and curled and just generally shone. "So it's a practice for when we do it for real."

"I find it helps people relax for the Big One," the pastor said as he walked over to his wife and gave her a quick kiss. "It'll only take us a minute to wrap up."

"Take your time."

Garrett frowned. Watching the pastor kiss his wife made him realize what he was missing. Those kind of affectionate kisses weren't part of his moves. When he kissed a woman, it was just a rest stop on the road to someplace else. That used to be enough for him.

"Actually, your husband has already given us lots to think about." Nicki shifted in her chair. "We could save the rest for later."

"Yeah," Garrett agreed quickly. He didn't like the feelings those questions stirred up. He'd been a perfectly happy single male a week ago. "I should go check the limo anyway."

Garrett got up from the chair and smiled a good-bye. He would have gone to check the *Titanic* if it would have gotten him out of the store, but no one needed to know that. They didn't even ask what he needed to check on the limo. It was a good thing, he told himself as he stepped out of the store, because he didn't need to check anything.

"I should go check on the twins, too," the pastor said to Nicki. "They're at Mrs. Hargrove's place. Her niece is taking care of them, and they can be a handful."

Nicki waited for the pastor to leave before she turned to Glory. "You don't happen to sell black spandex stuff in the store, do you?"

Glory shook her head. "We have black duct tape that stretches, but that's about all."

Nicki doubted Bonnie would wear duct tape.

"I do have the makeup, though," Glory said as she held up a paper bag. "You're welcome to pick out what you'd like to borrow. I hear you've got a big date coming up tonight."

Nicki nodded. "The Thanksgiving Eve service at church."

"Why, that's a good idea—I've been looking forward to the service ever since Matthew told me about it. I hear it's been a tradition in Dry Creek since the turn of the century."

"That's why people bring their own candles. Back in the early days, the church couldn't afford to buy any candles, and since the service was at night they needed light. The church didn't have electricity back then—actually, the church didn't even have a building. Everyone just met in the back room of Webster's store for services. I don't know who came up with the idea of people taking their candle to the front of the church and leaving it on the alter when they said what made them thankful.''

Glory nodded. ''Matthew told me the altar back then was made of a stack of cans set on top of some boxes. I can almost see those first candles in my mind. I've been thinking I might paint a scene of them—Elmer and Jacob told me there were all kinds of candles and candleholders. The cowboys sometimes just brought their candles in their tin drinking cup. That was all they had.''

''And Mrs. Hargrove has a silver candelabra that belonged to her mother—she says her mother bought it specially for the Thanksgiving service so she'd have enough candles to represent every member of her family.''

''Candlelight can be very romantic,'' Glory said as she opened the paper bag and rummaged around. ''I even put some perfume in here.''

''It's only a little bit of a date. He'll be gone after Thanksgiving.''

Nicki wondered if going out on a date with a handsome man who was leaving town was the smartest move a woman could make. She'd be forever comparing her dates with Lester to her one date with Garrett.

"Then you'll need a touch of lipstick, too," Glory said as she examined Nicki. "I think with your coloring we need to go with the rose."

"I'm not very good with the lines," Nicki confessed as she peered into the bag of cosmetics Glory had brought over. There were lipsticks and lip liners. Mascara and eye shadow. "What's that?"

"A pot of smudge for your cheeks—it adds some glitter."

"Won't I look kind of funny?"

"Not if you ask your mother to help you with it all."

"Oh." Nicki had almost managed to forget that her mother was here. "She and I don't have that kind of a relationship."

"Who knows what kind of a relationship you can have? Give it some time."

Nicki was going to point out that twenty-two years was a lot of time to give someone when they made no move to contact you, but she didn't get her mouth opened before she heard footsteps on the porch and the door of the store opened.

"There you are," Nicki's mother said as she entered the store and saw Nicki standing at the counter. "Garrett said you were here. I asked him to go into

Miles City to buy groceries and wondered if you would go with him.''

''We have enough groceries at the ranch.''

''Do you have a hundred and ten pounds of turkey and forty pounds of potatoes?''

''No, but we don't need those kind of groceries,'' Nicki said even as her unease grew.

''We do now,'' Nicki's mother announced with a flourish. ''Garrett said you didn't have plans for Thanksgiving dinner so I took the liberty of inviting guests.''

''You mean Mrs. Hargrove?'' Nicki hoped that was all her mother meant. That would be fine. She would have invited Mrs. Hargrove herself if they were having more than soup anyway.

''I mean the whole town of Dry Creek.''

''The whole town? That must be fifty, sixty people.''

''Seventy including me and Garrett. Eighty if we can reach everyone at the Elkton Ranch. Garth and his new wife, I think it is Sylvia, might have gone to Seattle—Jacob is going to call them and see. Even if they are not there, their ranch hands will probably like to come. I've never known a cowboy to turn down a turkey dinner.''

''We can't possibly—'' Nicki tried to calculate just how many turkeys that would be.

''Don't worry—everyone's helping. The kids at

the café agreed to bake the turkeys for us early to-morrow morning. And Jacob will help them bring them out to the ranch.''

''But we'd need pies and sweet potatoes and rolls—''

''We've got it organized. All you need to do is ride along with Garrett into Miles City to buy the food.''

''I haven't even dusted yet.'' Nicki wondered if there might not be something to say for living out of a truck like Garrett did. No one ever expected him to entertain.

''Everything will be fine,'' Nicki's mother said. ''We're not fussy.''

''You—not fussy? You made Dad use a coaster when he drank water at the kitchen table. And it was Formica. It was made for water spills.''

''That was a long time ago. And it wasn't water he was drinking. I thought if I insisted on a coaster he would think twice before he drank in front of you kids.''

''Oh.''

''A child's eyes see everything,'' Nicki's mother continued. ''I knew Charles would hate himself if you and Reno didn't grow up to respect him. Next to the land, you were all he had.''

''He had you.''

Nicki's mother winced. "There's more to the story than you know."

"Then tell me."

Nicki could feel her mother measuring her.

"It's not just about me. But if I can, I'll tell you. I have to ask someone's permission first."

"Is that why you're going to visit Dad's grave? To ask him if you can tell us it was all his fault?"

Nicki wondered if she was too old to run away from home. She had already lost her mother. She didn't want to have the memory of her father tarnished as well by hearing that he had displeased her mother because he drank too much. Even if her father had done that, her mother was probably the cause.

Another pair of footsteps sounded as someone stamped the snow off their shoes before opening the door to the hardware store.

"Everybody ready to go into Miles City," Garrett said as he rubbed his hands together. He'd heard Mrs. Hargrove give the food calculations and he'd joked that he shouldn't have left his truck in Las Vegas. He'd surprised himself when he'd joked. Usually a holiday meal like Thanksgiving gave him a headache. But sitting down with the bunch of people he'd met in this little town didn't seem so bad.

Garrett wondered if something was wrong with him. He'd lived his life by one rule—keep moving in life because then everyone stays a stranger. It was a good rule. That way he didn't disappoint anyone, not even himself. Odd, how that rule no longer sounded very appealing to him.

Chapter Nine

Nicki glittered. She could see it out of the corner of her eyes. She hadn't put on any of the "pot of smudge" Glory had loaned her so she must have gotten sugar on her cheek when Mrs. Hargrove, who had been making pies all afternoon, hugged her. The fortunate thing was that in the darkened church no one cared if Nicki glittered or glowed or downright sparkled like Garrett did.

The day had quieted down and the church looked elegant in the candlelight. The work for the day was done, and all was peaceful except the rustling of little feet in the back pews of the old church. The church walls were white but the flickering of the candles turned the walls golden. Long shadows stretched along the walls as people filed into the church.

Nicki was wearing a plain navy pantsuit with a very ordinary silver pin. She'd looked at the makeup Glory had lent her and quietly set it aside. She could dress up like she was a princess but that wouldn't make her one. She needed to keep her feet firmly planted and, for her, that meant looking the way she always had. She knew there were no fairy-tale endings, and she needed to remember that Garrett was going to leave soon.

The fact that she had dressed plainly didn't mean that Garrett had. He was wearing the tuxedo again and he looked every bit as handsome as he had early this morning.

Even without the limousine, he took Nicki's breath away. But it wasn't just the tuxedo or the limo. She would have found him handsome if he was wearing an old jogging suit and standing beside a bicycle. All of which was why Nicki needed to keep her feet planted in reality. It would be all too easy to let herself become too attached to him. She needed to keep her heart safe.

Nicki and Garrett were on their date. The people of Dry Creek had given them their own pew in honor of the occasion. At least Nicki assumed that was why everyone said hello to them but no one stayed to sit beside them.

The evening had transformed Dry Creek.

All afternoon, everywhere Nicki looked, someone

was chopping vegetables or peeling apples or grinding cranberries. She and Garrett had driven to Miles City and returned with enough bags of groceries to fill up the limousine. Nicki's mother had given them a wad of fifty-dollar bills, insisting the Thanksgiving dinner was on her.

By the time they got back to Dry Creek, the work teams were aproned and ready to go. Mrs. Hargrove took the ingredients for the pies and her helpers went with her to her house to bake. Jazz and Linda took the turkeys and the bread for the stuffing. Glory and Matthew were in charge of vegetables and took the bags of green beans, muttering something about hoping the twins liked to snap things.

Even Elmer had been put in charge of the butter when Lillian remembered he liked to carve. He was commissioned to shape the butter into five large turkeys with lines fine enough to show the feathers.

Nicki had volunteered to bake pies, but her mother said she and Garrett were needed back at the ranch to clean the main room in the bunkhouse and put up enough sawhorse tables to seat eighty people.

"We used to get over a hundred people in there when we had guests before," Lillian had said when Nicki had started to protest. "The room can't have shrunk. We get ten to a table and you can fit eight tables in there easy if you put them sideways where the beds used to go."

The bunkhouse had had cowboys sleeping in it for over a hundred years, and the metal legs of the beds left scars that still could be seen in the hardwood floors. Nicki supposed if you matched the bed markings you could get eight tables. There used to be sixteen beds, eight on each half of the bunkhouse.

Garrett drove Nicki back to the ranch in the limousine while her mother stayed in Dry Creek to help with the food.

If everyone hadn't been so intent on their tasks, Nicki would have suspected they had conspired to leave her and Garrett alone. But they didn't give the two of them a second glance when she and Garrett pulled out of town so Nicki decided they'd just paired Garrett with her because he looked strong enough to swing a sawhorse around. She would need that kind of help to set up the tables.

Once Nicki decided she and Garrett were just a work team, she didn't have any trouble talking to him. She'd started out where she'd usually start with a new ranch hand. She'd told him stories about the early days of the ranch. She even told him about the time the cowboys on the ranch had sent back East for a bride and then played poker all winter trying to decide who would get to woo the young woman first.

In turn, Garrett told her about some of the places where he'd driven with Big Blue—how the trees of

Tennessee were thick and green and the ocean off the Florida coast was pale blue in the morning.

It wasn't until they opened the closet and found the old pair of children's ballet shoes, however, that they started talking about themselves. Nicki had forgotten about the shoes. Her mother hadn't always been disappointed in her. When Nicki was small, she and her mother had loved to dance together in the kitchen, twirling on the old linoleum until they collapsed in a tangle of giggles. Somehow, after her mother left, Nicki had forgotten there were any good times. When Garrett responded by telling her about his dad dying of liver failure and all of the lonely days he had spent waiting for his father to be a father to him, they both knew they were friends.

Now that they were on their date, sitting in the church that was lit by candlelight, however, the ease of the friendship wasn't the same. Nicki couldn't think of a thing to say. Garrett in overalls was a lot easier to talk to than Garrett in a tuxedo.

"The flowers are lovely," Nicki repeated for the tenth time. She still didn't know when Garrett had slipped away in the grocery store to buy the two red roses. It must have been when she was asking the produce clerk how many yams eighty people might eat if they also had mashed potatoes. "And they're perfect in this vase."

Garrett hadn't stopped with the roses. He'd bought

a tiny glass vase that had room for the roses and for a single white taper candle.

His first thought had been to get the biggest vase and the biggest bouquet of flowers that the store had. But then he'd seen the vase that also doubled as a candle holder and he knew he'd found what Nicki would like the best.

"I've never had a prettier candle for the service." Nicki usually followed the old cowboy tradition of melting enough wax in the bottom of a cup to make a candle stick to it. She'd usually just used one of the half-melted, broken candles she kept in a kitchen drawer for when the electricity failed. It might be a white candle or a red candle left from a previous Christmas. But the candle had never been special, and she seldom had anything new to say when she stood up and listed what she was thankful for that year. Over the years she had usually mentioned the ranch or her 4-H calf or something. "I should have gotten a better holder for you."

Garrett grinned. "I'm happy with my cup candle."

Garrett hadn't been to church more than twice in his life and this was nothing like those two other experiences. There were no women in hats and no rustle of important people. People here came in old knit scarves that had been washed until they were all the same colorless gray. Some wore jeans with shiny knees and jackets that were frayed. But they all seemed humbly glad to be together. They smiled and shook hands with each other as though they were longtime friends. Garrett supposed they were.

He wondered why that thought depressed him. He might not have a roomful of friends, but he'd probably seen more different cities than anyone in the church here. That had to count for something. Besides, he could feel Nicki's arm as she sat beside him. He wasn't quite without friends.

Garrett inched a little closer to Nicki. When Nicki had showed him those ballet shoes this afternoon, he had realized that someone else had had a lonely childhood beside himself. Sharing with Nicki had made him feel less of a loner. He supposed it didn't change anything, but he'd realized he wanted Nicki to remember him when he was gone. Usually, he wanted the women he met to forget him as soon as he pulled out of town. But not Nicki.

Nicki wondered if anyone could see her blush in the candlelight. She didn't know if she had moved closer to Garrett or if he had moved closer to her, but she suspected it was she who had done the moving. There was something about the darkness that made her want to be closer to him.

Garrett looked around the small church. "I don't see Lester."

"He'll be a little late." Nicki wondered for the first time why Lester always came to church just as it was almost over. It was as though he wanted points for attending, but didn't really want to be there.

"Oh." Garrett wondered if he could get Nicki to leave the service before Lester arrived. No, he supposed not. Especially not now that it looked like it was going to start.

Mrs. Hargrove stood and walked to the piano beside the altar. The piano playing signaled the beginning of the service and everyone was looking forward as the pastor rose and went to stand behind the altar.

"Each year in Dry Creek, we come together as a community and give thanks for what we have." The pastor looked out over the group of people assembled and smiled.

"We started doing this in the late 1890s when the Redfern Ranch had a harvest dinner that brought everyone from miles around together. Before this town began, we moved the tradition to the back of Webster's store and called it our Thanksgiving Eve service. Today we celebrate here. No matter where it has been held, we have kept the same spirit of thankfulness. Together this community has survived droughts and depressions. Together we've seen good years and bad years. We've seen children born and grow up and move away. We've welcomed strangers and said goodbye to friends. Let's again be thankful for what this year has brought to us. Bring your candle in your own time and share with us what God has done for you.''

Garth Elkton and his new bride, were the first to come to the altar. They carried a candleholder made of dozens of old keys. One fat white candle rose from the key base.

''The kids in Seattle made this for us for tonight so we came back early,'' Garth said proudly. He'd met Sylvia while she was director of a youth center that helped troubled teenagers. ''We're thankful that they are doing well and are coming back this summer for a full six weeks. They told us that the old keys stand for old habits they are throwing aside.''

A murmur of approval went through the congregation as Garth lit their candle. The Seattle kids had been popular with the people of Dry Creek.

''And what about your new bride?'' someone yelled from the back of the church. ''What's she thankful for?''

''She's thankful for him,'' Nicki whispered to Garrett. Marriage had transformed Garth into a man who couldn't stop smiling, but Sylvia still told everyone she was the luckiest one. ''She found someone who shared her dream.''

''The camp for the kids.'' Garrett nodded. He had heard about the Seattle youngsters who were putting down roots in Dry Creek even though they had only been here for one month last winter. Many of the kids still wrote letters to the town of Dry Creek and the townspeople took turns writing back.

The next ones to bring their candles to the front of the church were the Curtis twins, the two six-year-old boys that belonged to the minister and his new wife. Their blond heads were bent as they carried two tin can holders to the altar. When they set the holders on the altar, their father reached out to light their candles from the main candle on the altar.

Nicki could see that the twins had made their candleholders from two identical aluminum cans. They had each cut out a figure in the can so the light from the candle would show through. One figure had wings and had to be an angel. The figure in the other can looked more like a mortal woman.

"We're thankful because we have two mommies now," the first twin boy said.

"And one of them's still an angel," the other boy added eagerly. "Mrs. Hargrove says. Our first mommy is our guardian angel and she flies over us with her supersonic wings that go zoom-zoom."

"All I said was that I'm sure she's watching out for you boys if there's any way she can," Mrs. Hargrove added from where she sat at the piano. "She knows that we need all the help we can get with that particular task."

The adults in the church smiled.

"And angels don't zoom around," Mrs. Hargrove added indulgently.

"They don't need to," one of the twins agreed. "They have those wings that fly like this." The twins demonstrated how angels fly as they flew back to the pew where they were sitting with their new mother, Glory.

"Those are the cutest little boys," Nicki whispered to Garrett.

He nodded in agreement.

Mrs. Hargrove left the piano and was the next one to bring her candles to the altar.

"Mrs. Hargrove brings candles for all of the Hargroves," Nicki whispered to Garrett as they watched the older woman bring two heavy silver candelabrum to the front. "I think she's up to twenty-two candles that she lights and for each one she mentions a relative by name."

"The Hargroves are grateful," Mrs. Hargrove began. "Two new babies in the family this year and Doris June is coming home next summer to stay for a spell with me."

A ripple of surprise went through the congregation.

"She might even open a business here," Mrs. Hargrove added proudly. "She's got quite a business head on her."

Mrs. Hargrove went on to announce the name of

each Hargrove family member as she lit the corresponding candle for them. By the time she had finished, the church glowed brighter inside.

Linda went to the altar next and lit a small green candle standing in a cup from the café. The candle was scented with pine and it started to give off its scent as soon as she lit it.

"I'm grateful for the café," she said quickly as she turned to walk back to her seat. "Business is good."

"And it will be even better with their new Romance Special," the pastor added from where he stood. "See me later for details."

Linda turned around and smiled at the pastor. "Thanks."

"We're determined to get that Jenkins' place bought." The pastor looked over the congregation. "Besides, a little bit of romance will be good for this town."

Everyone laughed and then grew silent.

Garrett watched the candles burn as others in the church brought up their candles. Before long there were candles of every color and size. And the holders were as individual as the people in this town. But almost all of the candle holders looked as if they'd been brought to the altar for many years and had followed the lives of their owners during the good and the bad of that time.

"I'm going to go up now," Garrett whispered to Nicki. "Do you want to come with me?"

Nicki nodded and Garrett didn't know when he'd been as proud. Nicki was willing to walk with him in front of the whole town.

Nicki felt her hand tremble slightly as she steadied her candleholder and took a quick look at the man beside her. The soft light of the candles played on Garrett's face and Nicki decided her first impression of him had been right. He was kind and handsome and—

"She's got flowers," a young girl said in awe when Nicki walked past. "And they're beautiful."

Nicki smiled down at the girl, Amy Jenkins. The six-year-old was clearly writing a story in her head about the flowers and the romance they implied. Nicki almost corrected her and then decided to let it be. Maybe there wasn't as much harm in fairy tales as she'd come to believe.

"You first," Garrett whispered when they reached the altar.

Nicki put her candle on the altar and lit it. Then she turned to face her friends. "This year I'm thankful for—" Nicki stopped. She always said the ranch. But the flowers seemed to promise more than land. She looked out at the candlelit faces around the church. So many of them looked back at her with hope and love on their faces. Why hadn't she seen it before? She might not have had her mother around to help her grow up, but she'd had dozens of mothers and fathers in this church. "I'm thankful for all of you."

"And him," Amy Jenkins whispered from her pew. "You have to be thankful for him."

Nicki knew who the little girl meant. "I'm thankful for everyone tonight."

"I hope she doesn't mean Lester," Garrett said out of the side of his mouth as they stood in front of the altar. "That man isn't good enough for you."

Nicki didn't think he needed to know who made the little girl's eyes sparkle. "It's your turn to light your candle."

Garrett hadn't noticed until he set the cup down next to Nicki's that he was using one of the mugs that advertised the hardware store. He turned around to face the people. "I'm thankful that I get to meet new people and travel to new places like Dry Creek."

A ripple of appreciation went around the pews.

"We're glad you're with us, as well," the pastor said as Garrett reached to light his candle. The pastor also turned to Lillian. "We have two special guests this Thanksgiving."

The warmth of the people in the church made Garrett bold and, when he and Nicki sat back down, he took her hand to hold. It wasn't much of a move.

He'd made bigger one's before and never given it a thought. But holding Nicki's hand seemed momentous.

He felt complete.

Everyone stood and, with Mrs. Hargrove playing the piano, sang "Amazing Grace." When the last chord of the song faded, everyone remained standing for a minute as though savoring the evening together.

"Now let's give your neighbors a hug and wish them a happy Thanksgiving," the pastor said. "Then go home and get some sleep. I understand we have ten turkeys waiting for us tomorrow—not to mention Mrs. Hargrove's apple pie."

Garrett was grateful that none of the townspeople had sat in the pew with Nicki and him. Nicki wouldn't have a question about who she should hug since he was the only one sitting next to her.

Nicki's hair smelled of lemon and strands of it gently tickled Garrett's chin while he hugged her. Garrett thought he heard Nicki give a soft sigh of contentment, but he couldn't be sure. Maybe it was just his heart giving the sigh. For the first time in his life, he felt at home.

Garrett kept Nicki in his arms. The townsfolk silently filed out of the church and soon they were the only two left inside. Still, he didn't want to let her go.

Nicki stirred. She was sinking and she couldn't

afford to. She was the one who would need to get on with her life when the fairy tale ended. She looked around the empty church. "Did you see Lester leave?"

Garrett frowned. "I didn't even see him come in."

"Oh, I'm sure he's here. I wanted to be sure he got an invitation for tomorrow."

Nicki stepped back farther so she could breathe easier. "I'll catch up with him before he leaves. People generally hang out for a few minutes outside and talk. He'll be there."

Garrett felt the cold as Nicki walked away from him. Did Lester even know what a lucky man he was? He followed her down the aisle of the little church and out into the cold dark night. There was no snow falling, but small drifts of snow stood at the edges of the spaces where the cars had parked.

"Brrr—" Garrett rubbed his hands together. Sharp tingles of cold ran up and down his fingers and, when he breathed, a white puff of air circled his head.

Clusters of people stood and talked together in the area where the cars were parked. The night sky was clear and as black as velvet. Garrett looked up and saw a million stars twinkling down at him.

"That's something, isn't it?" the pastor said as he came over to Garrett. "I never get tired of looking at all those stars."

Garrett grunted. "Makes the sky kind of crowded."

The pastor laughed. "I understand that when you get close to them, there's lots of room between the stars. Some might even think an individual star might be lonely. I imagine even a star wants company sometimes."

"Yeah, well." Garrett saw that Nicki had found Lester. He was standing over there talking to Elmer. The cold didn't seem to bother Lester and he had his coat open in the front as he talked. The man wore a plaid Western shirt.

Garrett frowned as he thought of the overalls he had waiting for him back at the ranch. All he had was either workclothes or the tuxedo. Neither one showed him off to his best advantage. He needed a sweater. Women always liked a man in a sweater.

"So, how's it going?" the pastor asked a little tentatively.

Garrett turned to look at the pastor square and forced himself to stop the frown. "She's gone to give Lester a personal invitation to Thanksgiving dinner. She didn't give anyone else a personal invite."

A couple of cars had turned on their headlights and the stars were no longer visible. But the people were a lot clearer and Garrett could even see Lester smile.

"Ahh."

"Not that it matters, I suppose. I'm heading out as soon as my cousin gets here anyway." Garrett pulled his eyes back away from Lester and looked at the pastor again.

"I see." The pastor nodded. "Well, then, I guess it's just as well she's inviting Lester. He's a solid man and he'll still be around."

Garrett snorted. "He's too old for her. Besides, she deserves somebody better."

Garrett could see that Nicki had turned and was walking back toward him. She was smiling so he assumed Lester was coming to dinner.

"Nicki deserves to be happy," the pastor agreed.

"He's coming," Nicki said when she came close to Garrett again. "I wanted to be sure he was coming because Reno should be back. Reno likes to have someone he can play cards with once the dishes are done."

"Oh, well." Garrett felt immediately better. "That's good he can come then."

If Lester kept Reno busy playing cards, Garrett would have even more time to talk to Nicki. He might even convince her to sneak out under the stars with him and dance a waltz or two. If they didn't freeze to death, it would be quite romantic.

"Maybe Chrissy will be here, too, by then," Nicki continued. "Maybe she and my mother can play bridge with Reno and Lester."

Garrett was beginning to like the sounds of Thanksgiving better and better all the time. It was all a matter of planning things.

"Well, I'd better get home and get the twins into bed so we can enjoy tomorrow." The pastor smiled as he turned to join Glory and his sons. He had only walked a couple of steps when he turned and looked at Garrett. "You know, you deserve to be happy, too. Don't sell yourself short. Think about it—we'll talk more later if you'd like."

Garrett almost automatically disagreed with the pastor. He wasn't selling himself short by knowing his limitations. He'd always believed happiness was too much to ask for and he was right. He was no good at things like marriage and forever after. His highest hope had only been to have short-term fun.

"What was that about?" Nicki asked.

"We'd been talking about the stars," Garrett answered with a small smile. He doubted the pastor knew about short-term fun. "I think he's trying to get them to move a little closer together."

"Oh. That doesn't sound very easy." Nicki frowned.

"He didn't say it would be easy." Garrett wondered if the star who stood beside him could be any prettier. The cold had turned Nicki's cheeks red and her eyes sparkled. "Come on, let's go home."

Nicki rode in the front of the limo with Garrett and Nicki's mother rode in the back.

"I never knew this road could ride so smooth," Nicki said as Garrett made the turn onto the Redfern Ranch property. "I wonder if Reno will let us trade the baler in and get a limo." But in spite of her words, she wondered if a limo would be the same without Garrett at the wheel.

"I wish I had Big Blue here so you could take a ride in her, too. She'll show you some smooth riding. Too bad she's back in Vegas at Chrissy's."

"I don't suppose you ever drive by Dry Creek when you're delivering your loads?" Nicki held her breath. She'd wondered about that more than once this evening. "You could stop in."

"There's not much trucking that goes by here."

"Oh." It was probably just as well, Nicki thought. It would be hard to settle down with someone like Lester if she kept remembering Garrett.

"You could meet me someplace when I'm in Vegas or Salt Lake City."

"Sure." Nicki doubted she would ever hear from Garrett after he left. She certainly wasn't going to hang out in either place hoping to catch him when he drove through. It sounded too depressingly like what her mother must have done years ago. Nicki wasn't like her mother, and she wasn't going to make the same mistake of leaving her land for the empty promise of excitement somewhere else.

Oh, well, Nicki thought to herself as she saw the house come into view. She might not have more than a memory, but it would be something to remember that she'd once had a date with Prince Charming. How many ranch women could say the same?

Somehow the thought of it didn't cheer Nicki like she thought it would. Regardless of what moment she had in her past, living a practical life day in and day out was sounding duller with each passing hour. At least things would return to normal when Garrett and her mother finally left.

"We're here," Garrett announced as he pulled the limo under the tree that had become its parking space. The dog, Hunter, seemed happy to share the area once he'd smelled the tires a few times this afternoon.

The kitchen was chilly when they came inside.

"Well, I'm tired," Nicki's mother announced. "If no one minds, I'm going to head up to bed."

No one minded. In fact, no one even noticed the smile Nicki's mother had on her face as she started up the stairs.

"I should be going to bed, too," Nicki said as Garrett helped her off with her coat. "Unless you'd like some tea?"

"I love tea." Garrett hoped no one ever got struck

down for lying. His fellow truckers would laugh themselves silly if they saw him drinking a cup of tea. He bet it was even herbal.

"Peppermint okay?" Nicki asked as she walked over to the counter.

"It's my favorite." Garrett figured as long as he was lying he might as well go all the way. And he could convince himself that peppermint tea was nothing but a liquid breath mint and a breath mint was a good dating move. Even a trucker would understand the need for a breath mint.

"Reno doesn't like it, but tea always warms me up on a cold night," Nicki said as she put the kettle on the stove and almost fanned herself without thinking. The night might be cold, but she didn't need warming up. What she needed was something to relax her and keep her sensible. In case the tea wasn't enough, Nicki also turned on the radio and started to move the knob. "How about some news?"

Garrett knew he didn't have much time to store up his memories of Nicki and there were many things they hadn't done together. Listening to the news wasn't top on his list of memories to make. In fact, it didn't even make it to the bottom of the list. "Here, let me find a station."

Garrett stepped over to the radio and turned the knob until he found what he wanted. The sounds of a slow-moving song softly filled the kitchen. "Care to dance?"

"In the kitchen?" Nicki stood with the kettle in her hand. She was ready to pour the hot water into the teapot.

Garrett shrugged. "We're on a date. We can dance anywhere."

Nicki set the kettle back on the stove. "I used to dance in the kitchen with my mother."

Garrett smiled. "I know. You told me."

Nicki knew she shouldn't dance in the kitchen. It was opposed to everything she had done with her life since her mother had left. It spoke of foolishness and dreams of impossible fantasies. It was definitely not sensible. "My dance shoes don't fit me anymore."

"It doesn't matter if you dance barefoot." Garrett held out his arms to her. "You can even dance in your boots if you want."

"I really shouldn't," Nicki said, but her feet betrayed her and she moved toward Garrett anyway. "I haven't danced in years."

Try twenty-two years, Nicki thought to herself as she melted into Garrett's arms. She'd avoided dances in high school for more reasons than because she'd never had a serious boyfriend. Dancing was for women like Nicki's mother, not for women like Nicki.

"I don't know how to dance," Nicki murmured

even as she felt her feet giving lie to what she was saying. Her feet were moving in rhythm with Garrett. She hadn't forgotten a thing about dancing over the years. Except— "My mother used to let me lead."

Garrett smiled into her hair. "I'm not your mother."

Oh, my, Nicki thought. She really should have that cup of tea. It would settle her stomach and make the butterflies leave. But Garrett pulled her even closer and she forgot about the tea.

By the end of the second song, Nicki had also forgotten about the ranch and the dinner tomorrow. She'd even forgotten that Reno was out on the road coaxing the old cattle truck home tonight. All she knew was that she was dancing with Prince Charming, and he was holding her like she was a princess to him.

Chapter Ten

Meanwhile, on the open road about ten miles from Dry Creek, Montana

Reno Redfern cursed turkeys everywhere. Or was it pilgrims he needed to curse?

He was lying on his back on the road embankment somewhere between Miles City and Dry Creek while looking up at the underside of his old truck. The ground was frozen solid beneath his back and oil was dripping on his forehead. And it was all because he was trying to get his truck running so he would be home for Thanksgiving.

Not that Nicki or he would be cooking any turkey. But he knew that it was important that he be home for his sister so that they could ignore the day together.

Before Reno had slid under his truck he had looked at his watch and it showed it was almost midnight. His first hope had been that someone would stop by and give him a ride into Dry Creek. From there he could call Nicki and she could come get him. But there wasn't much traffic on this road at noon during a busy day; he doubted there'd be any passing through at this hour the night before a holiday.

That leaking oil made him think there was engine trouble in the old truck. He wondered if they could find a used truck anywhere for a thousand dollars or so that would have enough power to get their cattle to market. He figured a thousand was as high as they could go unless they went into debt, and Redferns never went into debt.

Reno sighed. It wasn't always easy to have one's ancestors looking over your shoulder, but that's the way it had been for him and Nicki. If they even thought of doing something different, several kind souls in Dry Creek would remind them that the Redferns never did it that way.

The only thing the town had ever let them change was the Thanksgiving dinners the ranch used to hold for the whole community. Reno knew that was because they felt sorry for Nicki and him ever since their mother had abandoned them.

Reno felt the rumble of a vehicle coming down the road before he turned and saw the lights.

Hallelujah! Those lights were too high for a car so they must belong to a truck or at least a pickup. It was probably some farmer coming back from somewhere and that suited Reno just fine. A farmer wouldn't mind the smell of the oil that would hang around Reno even after he wiped the actual oil itself off of his forehead. Besides, Reno always had something to talk about with another man.

Reno heard the truck start to slow and so he figured he might as well try to plug that oil leak as best as he could. No sense leaving an oil spill like that on the ground. He'd already have to dig up the dirt around the oil or nothing would grow there for the next decade. Reno wadded up his handkerchief and jammed it up into the underbelly of the truck.

If Reno hadn't been concentrating on his handkerchief, he would have noticed earlier that the man had an awfully light footstep. And that he made a tinkling sound when he walked.

Not that Reno was in a position to be fussy about his company.

"Nice of you to stop—" Reno began as he slid himself out from under the old truck.

What the—? Reno was looking up into the night's darkness and there standing in front of the headlights was a woman who shone and glittered from the top of her low-cut dress to the bottom of its too-short hem. "What are you, an angel?"

Reno was prepared to die right then and there if she was. My, she was a sight to behold, all curvy and golden in the light.

"No," the woman said, and her voice started to tremble. "I'm a bride."

That's when Reno saw the tear that trailed down the woman's cheek. If there was anything that made him more nervous than a woman, it was a woman who was crying. "Ah, ma'am—"

Reno reached for his handkerchief—which was a futile thing to do considering he'd already used it to plug another leak. "Look, ma'am, don't cry. It's going to be okay."

"No, it's not." The woman started crying in earnest now. "He never did love me."

Reno figured he didn't know anything about angels and even less about crying women, but he did know one thing for sure. He pulled himself to his feet so he could say it square. "The man's a fool then if he can't see who you are."

"That's right," the woman said, and she took a shaky breath. Then she started to cry again. "But he's not the one who got be-betrayed."

Reno usually didn't feel comfortable when he met a new woman. He always worried that he had salad stuck in his teeth or that his conversation was boring or his hair was doing something funny. But this woman was so wound-up, she wouldn't notice if he had a tree growing out of his skull.

"That bad, huh?" Reno asked. He nodded sympathetically. "Then we'll just have to go get him."

The woman nodded a little uncertainly. "Get him?"

"Yeah, we could do a pie in the face. That's always good. Or maybe a kick in the seat of the pants. Or—"

The woman had stopped crying and was smiling just a little. "We could sell his name to a hundred telemarketers."

"That's the spirit."

"Or tell his new girlfriend what a creep he is."

Reno nodded. "Or we could drive into the next town of Dry Creek and get us a cup of coffee if the café is still open."

"Oh—" The woman smiled even wider. "Are we close to Dry Creek? I thought I'd never get there."

"You're going to Dry Creek? Not just through Dry Creek?"

The woman nodded. "Actually, I'm going to the Redfern Ranch near there to visit a friend."

Reno knew every friend Nicki had made since she was ten years old and none of them could be this vision in front of him. And he'd certainly know if she was a friend of his. That meant the woman was either truly an angel or she was thoroughly confused. Reno's bet was on confused. She probably had the Redfern Ranch mixed up with the Russell Dude Ranch that was located two counties away.

But stopping by the Redfern Ranch wouldn't make her late for seeing her friend whoever the friend was. Not even the cowboys would be up at the Russell Ranch at this time of night.

"What a coincidence! I'm going to the Redfern Ranch, too. Do you mind if I ride along?"

"Would you? I can't figure out where I'm going at night like this. There's not even any signs any-place."

"I'd be happy to show you the way."

Chapter Eleven

Garrett hadn't slept at all during the night. Instead he had lain on the sofa in the living room of the Redfern Ranch until a faint light started to seep into the windows. He just kept asking himself if what he felt was happiness. He'd never expected to be happy in life and he didn't quite know what to make of it.

The feeling had started last night when he and Nicki waltzed around the kitchen floor. They hadn't talked much; they'd just snuggled together and moved to the music.

It was the feeling of belonging that made him first suspect it was happiness. Garrett had never belonged anywhere, not even when he was growing up with his father. They hadn't had a home; they had only had an address. Garrett wandered the streets and his father drank. His father never acted as if Garrett belonged at home. In fact, he always seemed surprised to see him there.

When Aunt Rose had mentioned taking him into her home when he was sixteen, Garrett had been terrified. A real home with a real family was foreign to him. He'd felt awkward, as though he would be all elbows in a place like that. And he hadn't gotten any better. But here he was. Longing for something that scared him spitless.

It was all Nicki's fault.

He hadn't been happy, but he'd at least been content before he met her.

The one dependable thing about going from place to place as a trucker was that he was safe. There was no one to disappoint him and no one he could disappoint. He didn't have to say any goodbyes because no one ever expected him to stay anyway. It wasn't the best way to live, but it didn't involve any risk to his heart, either.

And now there was Nicki. She had become home to him and he'd never be safe from heartache again.

Well, Garrett told himself, there was no sense in brooding about it. A man didn't break trucking records because he believed in taking the slow route. There was no going back to the way things were. Nicki had danced her way into his heart, and the only way he knew to remove her was to prove to himself that she wouldn't marry him if he were the last man on the earth.

He figured that's pretty much how it would stack up if she chose Lester over him.

Garrett shifted the pillow under his head and eased farther into the sofa. There was no point in getting up yet. He'd lie here and try to figure out how to ask Nicki to marry him so that he could make a quick getaway when she said no.

Knowing he couldn't stay once she'd rejected him meant he'd have to wait until after the dinner to ask Nicki anything. He couldn't leave her with all of those people to feed and it would be uncomfortable for both of them to work together after she'd said no. Lester sure wasn't the kind of guy to stay around and help with the dishes so Garrett had already decided he'd be the one with his hands in the hot water.

Given the number of people coming for dinner and the amount of pots and pans that would be used, Garrett figured he had a good ten hours left of this happy feeling. Maybe he should get out a piece of paper and write down how it felt so he could read it to himself when he was old and gray.

Now that was a depressing thought.

Upstairs, Nicki stared at the ceiling. She'd been afraid to sleep. She knew if she started to dream she would see the real face of Prince Charming in her dreams. Hadn't she read somewhere that if a person died in their dream, they died in real life? Well, it probably wasn't true. But why chance it? The very least that would happen is that her dream would dissolve into tears, and she didn't want that to happen.

Her dreams might have been annoying to her before last night, but at least they weren't self-tormenting nightmares that involved a lot of tears and gnashing of teeth.

The dark in her room got a very little bit lighter. In a few minutes, the darkness would be tinged with pink and Thanksgiving Day would begin. At least the kitchen would be crowded with all kinds of people before too long. There would be no time for quiet dancing with Garrett so she wouldn't have to worry about stopping herself from asking him to dance with her again.

Nicki sat up when she could see the pink of the sun outside her window. Maybe if she got up and fixed some coffee she would feel better. There was no mail today so Lester wouldn't be coming by, but the coffee would settle her stomach anyway.

Nicki tightened the belt on her chenille robe as she tiptoed down the stairs. She didn't want to wake either Garrett or her mother. The day would be long enough even if it started an hour later.

The staircase in the old house went from the second floor hallway to the kitchen and Nicki was grateful for the fact. Garrett was asleep on the sofa and she didn't want him to know that she hadn't been able to sleep. She supposed he was used to nights like last night, but she wasn't.

Nicki almost expected the kitchen to be changed when she got down the stairs and looked up. But there was no golden web covering the room and no sprinkling of fairy dust on the counter. The refrigerator was still old and gurgling. The sink by the window was chipped and the faucet still needed replacing. There was no sign whatsoever that a fairy tale had been born here last night.

At least the coffeepot still sat on the counter by the sink and Nicki walked over to fill the unit with water. Her feet were bare and the linoleum was icy cold so she hurried to reach the rug in front of the sink.

Nicki turned the faucet and the water line hiccuped once before water started to pour out. She put the pot under the faucet before she looked out the window. The night was still dark and no snowflakes were falling like they had been yesterday morning. But— Nicki peered out the window more closely—what was that?

The limousine was parked under the old tree, but there to the side of the limo was a big shadow of something that was as high as the lower branches on the tree.

The pot wasn't full of water yet, but Nicki pulled it away from the stream of water and set it on the counter. She wasn't going to question her sanity again over something strange appearing in the night. She'd just get her broom handle and go investigate.

"Good morning," Garrett said from the doorway that opened into the living room. He had heard Nicki's footsteps and then the sound of running water. "How are you this morning?"

"Well, I'm not crazy," Nicki said firmly as she walked toward the coat rack beside the refrigerator. "I'm going to do what I should have done when you were out there and take the broom to it—whatever it is."

"Okay." Garrett wasn't so sure about her not being crazy. Not that it mattered when she was so cute in that robe of hers. "Chickens get out or something?"

Nicki had wrapped a knit scarf around her neck by the time Garrett walked over to the door. He'd at least had the sense to put a shirt and his overalls on as well as his shoes.

"That broom'll flatten a chicken." Nicki had picked up the broom handle she'd greeted Garrett with yesterday morning. "Maybe you need to take something smaller."

"There's some funny thing out there." Nicki

waved toward the window. "Looks like a truck with only its nose."

Garrett took four big steps to the window. "That's Big Blue."

"Your truck? I thought it was still in Vegas."

"It was." Garrett wondered if Nicki would let him borrow her broom. "And the reason it's only the nose is because she's not hooked up to a load. She shouldn't be here."

"Well, do you think someone stole it?"

Garrett nodded. "And she'd better have a good reason."

"I'll let you know," Nicki said as she finished wrapping the scarf around her neck.

"You're not going anywhere." Garrett put his hand out for the broom handle. "You shouldn't be out investigating strange things anyway. What if there was something dangerous?"

"Well, it's no better for you to be out there if there's trouble."

Garrett kept his hand outstretched. "Yes, it is."

Nicki's chin went up. "Just because you're a man—"

"It's not because I'm a man," Garrett said as he looked down at Nicki's feet. "It's because I've got shoes on my feet."

"Oh." Nicki handed him the broom handle. "I

forgot you wanted to be every woman's hero anyway.''

Garrett grinned as he took the broom handle and grabbed a jacket off the coat rack. Nicki's eyes were sparking again. ''Not every woman's hero. Just yours, sweetheart.''

Garrett was out the door before Nicki had her breath back. Sweetheart. She'd never thought she liked any of those ''darling'' names that men called women. Lester had called her Pumpkin once and she'd snapped his head off. But ''sweetheart'' was kind of nice. At least it didn't call to mind something that was fat and orange.

Nicki decided she'd take some of the coffee cake out of the freezer so she, Garrett and Lillian could have a nice breakfast before they started getting ready for the dinner. It was something she would have done for any other guests.

The fact that she could already hear herself humming while she made the eggs, well, that was just a holiday thing.

Outside, the temperature had to be close to zero degrees. Garrett had put the jacket on the second he walked out the door and he had still felt his breath catch in his throat. The ground cracked beneath his shoes because of all the frost.

Big Blue was darker than the just-dawning sky, but Garrett could easily make out the white letters of

Hamilton Trucking on the driver's door. Chrissy had done a good job of parking the truck beside the limo. There wasn't that much room between the car and the fence and Big Blue fit in snugly.

Maybe Chrissy had learned a thing or two about driving since he'd given her those quick two lessons in Vegas in case she needed to move Big Blue while he was gone. Of course, she didn't have a trucker's license. It was a fool thing to just take off in Big Blue.

Garrett put his hand on the door of Big Blue. It was cold enough to give a man frostbite. The windows were all frosted over. He hoped Chrissy had had the sense to turn on the small heater he had in back by the bed. If she had, she'd have been comfortable enough for the night.

Garrett knew Nicki's broom handle wouldn't do him any good in a fight, but he felt better keeping it with him anyway. At least if he had the broom, Nicki wasn't going out chasing something else. So he pulled the broom up with him as he opened the door to Big Blue and stepped up.

The night was still dark and Garrett couldn't see much inside of the truck's cab. There was nothing wrong with his hearing, however, and he definitely heard two grunts of surprise. One of them was Chrissy. The other was from a man.

She's gone and brought Jared with her, Garrett

thought to himself as he plastered a smile on his face. He was going to have to be cordial to that man if it killed him

"Garrett," the wail came from Chrissy, and Garrett saw movement in the bed area.

"Come in and shut the door," Chrissy said as she hugged a jacket to her and moved closer to the front seats in the truck. She was dragging half of the blankets with her. "It's freezing out there."

Garrett sat in the driver's seat and closed the door. He set the broom handle in the passenger's seat and turned around.

"I hope you and Jared had a good night's sleep." Garrett put his smile back on. He could be pleasant.

"I slept like a baby," Chrissy said sweetly. "I doubt Jared slept at all if he heard the things we were plotting to do to him last night."

"We?" Garrett made the connection as he looked at the other form in the bed. Jared didn't have a muscle to spare on his body and the arm that was reaching up to pull the rest of the blankets back had muscles to spare.

"What do you mean 'we'?" Garrett whispered as he took back the broom handle. "Who's here with you?"

"Well," Chrissy said as she yawned, "I couldn't find the place, you know. Dry Creek isn't on any of the maps I got in Salt Lake. I thought there would be signs, but no. I was lucky that his truck had broken down and he needed a ride.''

''That's a hitchhiker back there?'' Garrett wondered what decade he was in. Any sensible woman knew not to pick up a hitchhiker in this day. Especially on a back road in Montana. Especially at night. ''What were you thinking?''

Didn't his cousin watch the news?

''Well, he's not really a hitchhiker. I mean, I know I gave him a ride and all, but—''

Garrett was no longer listening to Chrissy. ''Why don't you go in the house and wait for me?''

''But he belongs here. It's not like I just picked up someone,'' Chrissy protested as she crossed her arms and refused to move.

The man in the bed swung his legs around and put his hand on Chrissy's arm. ''That's okay. I want to ask him what he's doing with Nicki's broom anyway.''

''You know Nicki?'' Garrett frowned. This man looked as if he would be a whole lot more trouble than that Lester fellow. He had a faint smear of oil on his forehead and the air of a man used to taking charge.

The man nodded. ''I'm her brother.''

''Reno?'' Garrett's frown turned to a smile. ''Well, why didn't you say so? She's been waiting for you.''

The man grunted. "I'm surprised Hunter let you get this close to the truck."

"Hunter's a good dog, but I think he's given up on biting me."

The man grunted again but he didn't smile. "Well, tell Nicki we'll be inside in a minute."

Garrett noticed that Chrissy wasn't making any move to leave with him. He wasn't sure he liked the possessive air that Reno had with Chrissy, but his cousin didn't seem to mind it.

"Well, I'll see you inside then." Garrett opened the door again.

The air wasn't any colder than when he had walked across the ranch yard a few minutes ago, but Garrett noticed it more. Hunter didn't even bother to follow him to the door.

Nicki met him at the door. "Was it Chrissy?"

Garrett nodded as he stepped into the kitchen. "And Reno."

"My brother?" Nicki asked in surprise. "What are they doing together?"

"I don't know, but I intend to find out." Garrett stomped the snow off his shoes as he stood on the mat just inside the door. "It's not like Chrissy to just pick up with some man."

"Reno's not just some man," Nicki protested as she ran her fingers through her hair. She had managed to comb her hair before she came down to the kitchen this morning. "And you don't need to take that tone. Reno's shy with women."

Garrett snorted. "He didn't look shy to me."

"You're sure it's Reno out there?"

"Hunter seems to like him."

"Well, that's Reno then," Nicki said as she moved and stood in front of the sink and looked out the window. The morning had grown lighter and she could see clearly as the door to Garrett's truck opened and Reno stepped out. "Maybe you just missed that he's shy."

Nicki saw Reno turn and offer his arm to the woman who stood behind him. Garrett was right. Reno didn't look the least bit hesitant as he helped the woman out of the truck cab. And she was wearing Reno's jacket.

Nicki didn't know her mother was up until she heard the sound of footsteps on the stairs. She turned.

Lillian Redfern stood in the stairway and she was fully clothed. She was wearing a red pants suit with matching lipstick and had her blond hair perfectly combed. "Did I hear you say Reno's shy with girls? I can't believe Charles Redfern's son would turn out shy."

"He's not just Dad's son. He's your son, too."

"What are you saying? That Reno's shy because of me?" Lillian Redfern laughed. "I don't have a shy bone in my body."

"Maybe Reno would have gotten to know that if you'd stayed around long enough for him to know you."

"Oh."

Nicki turned away from her mother and opened the door for Reno and Chrissy.

"It's cold out there," Chrissy said as she stepped inside the doorway, rubbing her hands. "Is it going to ever warm up?"

"It'll be warmer by the time everyone comes for dinner," Nicki said as Reno followed Chrissy in.

"People are coming for dinner?" Reno asked as he turned to close the kitchen door. "You invited people?"

"I'm the one who invited them," Lillian Redfern said as she stepped into the center of the room.

"Mom?" Reno asked quietly.

"Lillian is just staying for a few days," Nicki rushed to reassure everyone. "And she wanted to do one of the Thanksgiving dinners like we used to do— you know, where everyone in town comes over."

"Everyone in town?" Chrissy looked shocked. "You invited a whole town for Thanksgiving dinner?"

"Well, a few people are away at this time of year." Lillian kept smiling brightly. "It'll be fun. The only thing we have to do this morning is grind the cranberries and then set up the tables."

"The whole town?" Chrissy still looked shocked. "That's ten times worse than a wedding reception."

"We used to do it all the time," Lillian said. "Charles insisted. He loved to have people around."

"No, he didn't," Nicki said as she turned to get some plates out of the cupboard. "After you left, he stopped seeing everyone, even Jacob." She turned to her mother. "He even stopped going to church. You ruined his life."

"I didn't tell your father to stop going to church." Lillian walked to the sink. "That was his decision. Now, I'm going to have some coffee. Would anyone else like some?"

"You're not even sorry you left," Nicki said tightly.

"I wish you could understand how it was. I couldn't stay here. Not after—" Lillian broke off. "I still need to ask—"

"I know," Nicki said. "You need to ask someone if you can tell us."

"It's the truth." Lillian took a deep breath. "In the meantime, is there anything I can do to help with breakfast? I'm assuming everyone is hungry."

Nicki turned to the coffeepot. The day would be spent feeding hungry people. For the first time, she was glad her mother had invited the whole town to dinner. With all the people around, Nicki had a chance of forgetting her mother was here.

''I'll do the eggs,'' Garrett offered as he walked to the stove. ''Just give me a pan and I'm set.''

Nicki wondered how many people would need to be coming to dinner for her to forget Garrett was here.

Chapter Twelve

The inside of the bunkhouse was still musty so Nicki opened both of the doors. "It smells like old boots in here. Let's hope the air's better by the time people are ready to eat dinner."

The wood floor in the bunkhouse had been scrubbed clean yesterday and the windows had been washed.

Garrett had a sawhorse slung over his shoulder and he was walking to the end of the bunkhouse. He was wearing his farmer overalls and one of Reno's plaid flannel shirts. His hair was messy and straw dust had fallen on his neck when he took the sawhorse out of the barn. He looked more like a beggar than a prince.

And yet Nicki had to keep recounting the black scars on the floor where the bedposts had stood. They needed the information to place the sawhorses correctly for the tables. One moment Nicki would have all of the numbers straight and then Garrett would bring in another sawhorse and she'd lose track of her numbers because she was watching him.

It was, Nicki decided, only because everyone in Dry Creek had made such a fuss about them dating that she was distracted like this. It would pass. She just needed some cold air.

"I still say your mother is worried about something," Garrett said as he set down the sawhorse on scars number three and five. "Give her a little bit of time."

"I'm not telling her to leave," Nicki said as she braced herself to push open one of the windows that years of rain had warped shut.

Garrett snorted. "You're not asking her to stay, either."

Nicki tried to force the window open. It stayed shut. "She doesn't want to stay. She just wants some kind of cheap forgiveness and then she'll be on her way."

"She spent six hundred and ten dollars on Thanksgiving dinner. That's not cheap. She could have just sent a card or something."

"I wish she would have."

Garrett walked over and opened the window for Nicki. Cold air blew in. "Well, I can't say as I've done any better with my parents. Sitting in church last night, I wondered if I didn't need to do some forgiving of my own.''

Nicki looked out the window. The yard outside the bunkhouse was rough. Reno had driven the truck through this area during the last muddy spell and the tire tracks had frozen in place and were now covered with a light layer of snow. A few stalks of dried wildgrass poked through the snow here and there. There was nothing pretty about the ranch or her family. ''It's God's fault, you know.''

''Huh?''

Nicki turned to look at Garrett. ''Our whole family went to church. My father, my mother, me and Reno. It was supposed to keep everything safe. God shouldn't have let this happen to our family.''

''I know,'' Garrett said and opened his arms to Nicki. He didn't know, of course. He'd never given God much thought until last night. He'd never prayed in his life. But now. ''Maybe we should talk to the pastor about this.''

Nicki had her nose buried in flannel. Garrett's arms were around her. She didn't know why those two facts only added to her misery. ''I don't need any sympathy.''

''Who said the pastor will give you sympathy?''

''I mean from you.'' Nicki blinked back her tears and pulled herself away from Garrett's arms. She would do much better with a man who wasn't so kind. "I don't need all this—" Nicki waved her hands "—understanding."

Garrett frowned.

"I really can do fine by myself," Nicki said as she stepped back to the bedpost scars. "I think the next sawhorse goes on scars eleven and thirteen."

Nicki didn't even look up as Garrett walked out of the bunkhouse. She didn't want him to see the tears that were shining in her eyes.

Garrett rubbed his hands together as he opened the door to the barn. The day was warming, but it was still cold enough outside that he should have gloves. He kept a pair in Big Blue so he walked over to the truck.

Once he'd backed Big Blue up a few times earlier this morning, he'd forgiven Chrissy for driving her up here. The truth was he was glad to have the truck here so he could drive her away after his proposal. He figured that if Nicki wouldn't even let him comfort her, she surely wasn't going to agree to be his wife.

Garrett opened the door to Big Blue's cab and climbed up into her. He'd always liked sitting up high when he was driving down the road. He supposed that someday the fact that he was a trucker would once again be enough for him.

Ah, there were the gloves. Garrett reached into the

rear of the cab. As he picked the gloves up off the ledge by the bed, something small and hard fell to the floor.

"What the—?" Garrett twisted in his seat so he could lean over and see what had fallen.

He picked up the engagement ring. He recognized it. The last time he'd seen it had been when it was on Chrissy's finger back in Las Vegas.

Garrett knew the engagement ring Lillian had wanted to return to Charles was sitting on top of the refrigerator in the Redfern kitchen, but he would not have confused the two rings anyway. Even with the opals that surrounded it, the diamond in Lillian's ring was modest. Chrissy's diamond, on the other hand, was so large Garrett figured it had to be fake. Chrissy's fiancé, Jared, had lots of flash, but wouldn't have much money until that trust fund he'd talked about kicked in.

Holding the ring in his hand, Garrett realized something. A man didn't just walk up to a woman and ask her to marry him. He had to have a plan. He needed words. And maybe a flower or a strolling guitar player. A man didn't just wring out the dish rag after doing the Thanksgiving dishes and ask a woman to spend the rest of her life with him.

Even if a man expected the answer to be no, his dignity required that he give the matter some planning.

Garrett climbed down from Big Blue. Chrissy and Reno were in the house now sorting through trays of silverware with Lillian. At least Garrett had some time alone to think about a proposal.

The air inside the barn was warmer than the outside air and Garrett flexed his hands for a minute before he picked up another sawhorse. Nicki's horse, Misty, was in her stall and looked over at Garrett hopefully.

"Sorry, I don't have anything for you," Garrett said as he put the sawhorse down and walked over to rub Misty's forehead lightly. The mare whinnied softly and leaned her head closer to his hand. "That'a girl. I don't suppose you have any idea how to propose to someone?"

Misty lowered her head and blew air out her nose.

"Yeah, I don't, either." Garrett ran his hand over Misty's neck and gave her a pat. "It shouldn't be all that hard—I should just walk up and say, 'Will you marry me?'"

Misty nudged at his hand.

"Yeah, you're right—that's too direct. A woman probably wants something more."

Misty nudged his hand again.

"Yeah, you want something sweet, don't you? I suppose that's what a woman wants, too. Something sentimental." Garrett thought a moment. "I was never very good at that kind of thing."

Garrett heard someone open the barn door.

Chrissy stepped into the barn and slammed the door shut. "Men."

Garrett perked up. Chrissy would know more than a horse did about marriage proposals. "Troubles?"

Chrissy folded her arms and grunted.

"Well, I guess no one has proposed today yet, huh?"

Chrissy looked at him as if he'd lost his mind.

"I mean, I was thinking about when Jared proposed to you. Did he do something special? Something that you remember?" Garrett noticed his cousin was wearing a plaid shirt that looked like it belonged to Reno, too. How many flannel shirts did the man have?

Chrissy scowled at him. "Look, you don't have to find out anything more about me and Jared for Mom. I'm not getting married to Jared. She can relax."

"Well, good. I mean, not good that you're upset, but good that you're— Well, anyway, I'm not asking the question about how he gave you the engagement ring for your mom. I'm asking for, you know, general reference."

Garrett knew now why he didn't lie. He wasn't any good at it.

"He put it in a box and gave it to me."

"But did he say anything? Did he get down on

his knees or anything?'' Garrett would have to remember the knee thing. He might be able to do that.

''He said, 'Here it is,' and turned the television
on.''

''Oh.'' Garrett didn't think that would work so
well. ''But he'd probably said something romantic
earlier?''

''He asked if I wanted to order in pizza.''

''Well, I see. Thanks.'' Garrett supposed there was
no point in studying the technique of a man who had
obviously lost his fiancée anyway.

''The man's a jerk who deserves to be buried up
to his neck in an anthill. Nonpoisonous, of course.
Reno says the revenge thing can only be something
nonlethal.''

Chrissy turned as the barn door opened again.
Reno stepped inside.

Reno and Chrissy just looked at each other. Garrett
cleared his throat then he gave a final pat to Misty's
forehead. ''I'll be taking another sawhorse to the
bunkhouse.''

No one seemed to care.

Nicki had opened all of the windows by the time
Garrett brought in the sawhorse, and she was dusting
the shelves along the side of the bunkhouse.

''Got anything sweet for Misty?'' Garrett set the
sawhorse down.

''I thought we'd save her sugar for this afternoon.

The Curtis twins like to ride her and she always expects a treat for that. Can't say that I blame her—they want her to be a dragon. Besides, if the twins ride her, all the other kids will want a turn, too.''

"Sounds like she's going to be busy."

"We're all going to be busy." Nicki stopped dusting for a moment. "I saw you check out your truck. I hope it's okay. I mean, the gears and all."

"It's fine."

"It's just that if there was a problem with anything we'd be happy to help you get it fixed. Between the two of us, Reno and I have fixed almost every kind of engine there is."

Nicki knew it was a long shot that there was trouble with Garrett's truck, but she was hoping he'd have a reason to stay for a few more days, and any kind of mechanical trouble would be enough reason for that.

"No, Big Blue's fine." Garrett leaned against the sawhorse. "But what about your truck—do you need any help with it?"

Garrett didn't suppose help with a truck qualified as a romantic gesture, but it was a start.

Nicki shook her head. "We can't even order parts for the truck anymore. We'll have to buy something else when we can."

"Oh. Well, if you need anything hauled in the

meantime, let me know. I could even haul cattle for you if I got the right trailer to attach to Big Blue.''

''There's no more cattle sales this year.''

Garrett started to walk back to the door. ''Well, I'll go get the rest of those sawhorses. And then I'll start on the plywood tops.''

The plywood boards had been cut to serve as tabletops to go with the sawhorse bases twenty-some years ago but they were still sturdy. Nicki's father had wrapped a tarp around them when he stored them in the barn so they weren't even that dusty.

''But we must have had tablecloths when we used those tables before,'' Nicki said to her mother. Nicki and Garrett had gone into the kitchen to talk to Lillian. ''Even I remember white tablecloths.''

Lillian shook her head. ''Those were sheets. I'd gotten ten extra flat sheets to use.''

Nicki groaned. ''I wondered why there were so many flat sheets—I gave them away to the church rummage sale years ago. You should have said something when you left.''

''About the sheets?''

Nicki nodded stubbornly. ''You should have told me things like that that I would need to know. I wasn't prepared.''

''I know,'' Lillian said softly as she reached out

to put her hand on Nicki's shoulder. "And I'm sorry."

Nicki turned away without looking at her mother. "Well, we can't just eat off the plywood. We'll just have to think of something else. I think we have four or five sheets. Of course, they're all different colors and sizes."

Lillian withdrew her hand.

"Well, it doesn't have to be sheets," Garrett offered cautiously after a moment of silence. "I have lots of maps in Big Blue. We could use them for table covers."

"But they're your maps. You'll need them."

"I have too many maps," Garrett said and realized it was true. "Besides, most of the places I go these days are clearly marked on the freeways."

When had his life become so predictable? Garrett wondered. There was no more adventure in driving from Las Vegas to Chicago than there was in driving from Atlanta to St. Louis. It was all just following a path of freeways. If a robot could reach the gas pedal, he could drive Big Blue.

The maps were the perfect table covering, Nicki concluded in satisfaction when she stood up and admired the ten tables. She'd just finished taping the last of the maps to the plywood tabletops and they looked good. All of the lines and the tiny blocks of color here and there in the maps made the bunkhouse look happy.

Nicki looked more closely at the map on the table closest to her.

"What's this?" Someone had drawn lines with a red pen.

Garrett came over to look and started to chuckle. "Oh, that was a hurricane from a couple of years ago. I had to reroute myself all over the place."

"And this?" Nicki pointed to something written in green.

"Oh, that was my sunshine route. I was determined to work my way down to Florida for Christmas that year. I decided I wanted to see an alligator. Had to take loads to five states to do it, but I made it. Pulled into Florida Christmas Eve and met an alligator on Christmas Day."

Nicki looked at the other maps on the tables. The maps were taped together and wrapped around the edges of the table. She walked from table to table. All of the maps had lines drawn on them. "We can't use your maps. They'll get all dirty."

"That's fine." Garrett looked up from the folding chair he was fixing.

"You don't understand—I don't mean just a little dirty, I mean gravy-and-cranberry-sauce-spilled-on-them dirty. They'll be ruined."

Garrett shrugged. "Then we'll throw them away."

"But you can't—these maps tell all about your trips."

"I can get new maps and add new trips." Garrett snapped the chair into place and stood. "You know how it is—new horizons and all."

"I wish I did know how that is," Nicki said. Her voice was glum. She had such a tight hold on the past, she couldn't even see the future. She'd even been a little superstitious about going too far outside of Dry Creek. It was as though she thought that if she went someplace else, she couldn't come back. "The furthest I've been is Billings."

"Well, you could—" Garrett stopped himself. Was he going to say, *come with me?* He cleared his throat. "If you're interested in traveling, I could give you a list of good places to see."

"I've never seen an alligator." Nicki thought a moment. She hadn't realized how much she had missed. "Or a crocodile. Or a whale."

"You'll want to start on one of the coasts then."

Nicki nodded. Maybe she needed to buy an encyclopedia of sea animals. Just in case she ever got a chance to see one.

Someone stomped his boots lightly on the porch outside the bunkhouse door. Then Reno opened the door.

"She—" Reno jerked his head toward the house "—wants to know if you're all set out here. They called from the café and asked if it was time for the turkeys to be brought out.''

Garrett snapped the last chair into place. ''We're set for eighty people.''

Nicki looked around. She'd lit a couple of pine candles and the air in the bunkhouse now had a light holiday scent. The windows sparkled. The wood floor shone. The chairs were neatly lined up around each of the ten tables. ''We're ready.''

''And we're using paper plates?'' Reno stepped over to Nicki and asked quietly. ''She's okay with that?''

Reno didn't need to say who ''she'' was.

''I don't think she knows we have her china packed away,'' Nicki said. She had shoved the boxes even farther back into the walk-in closet that hung off the side of the bunkhouse. ''I thought she'd ask, but she hasn't. She always used to say a lady needed her china.''

Garrett was of the opinion that all a lady needed was a pair of emerald eyes, but he doubted Nicki wanted to hear that so he shuffled two of the chairs. ''We got the extra-thick paper plates.''

Reno nodded. ''Works for me. I was just wondering.''

''I'm surprised she never came back for the china.'' Nicki avoided looking in the direction of the closet. ''Dad said she bought that china with the egg money, one piece at a time. It took her five years to get all of the pieces.''

''Well, people's taste changes, I guess.'' Reno shrugged.

''I guess,'' Nicki agreed, but she wasn't really sure. Her mother's taste had been for pretty things back then and, as far as Nicki could tell, it was pretty things that her mother still wanted. Even this Thanksgiving dinner. It was some sort of pretty fairy tale all wrapped up in neighborhood cheer. Her mother couldn't just make a quiet apology and drive away like a normal person. No, she had to make a production of the whole thing with tears and hugs and cranberry sauce.

''She's not giving any speeches, is she?'' The thought suddenly struck Nicki. ''I mean the food is the whole thing, isn't it? She's not planning to apologize for stealing the money and leaving and everything again, is she?''

''She apologized for leaving?'' Reno frowned.

''Well…'' Nicki thought for a moment. ''She sort of implied an apology. Then she made it sound all mysterious and said it involved someone else—she as good as said she did it because Dad was a heavy drinker back then. Dad wasn't a drinker.''

''He was around the time when Mom left.''

''How do you know that? You were only four years old.''

Reno shrugged. "He drank some here and there for years. But it used to be worse. After Mom left, he cut back."

"Well, see—then it was because of her. When she left, he cut back."

"He cut back because of us. Without Mom, there was no one but him to take care of us."

She nodded. She wondered what their life would have been like if her mother had been willing to stick with her father in spite of his drinking. She supposed a drinking husband did not fit in with her mother's picture of a perfect life and so she just left.

Nicki looked down. She had a film of gray dust over her jeans. "Now that the room is ready, I guess we should all get ready, too."

Nicki wondered if she and Reno could ever be ready for this dinner their mother wanted.

Chapter Thirteen

"**M**ore yams?" Mrs. Hargrove leaned across the table and offered the dish to Nicki. "They're good for you."

Mrs. Hargrove had pronounced every item on the table as good for a person, even the butter in the turkey molds that Jacob had carved and the rolls that had been left too long in the oven and gotten hard and crusty.

"I'm stuffed," Nicki said.

"How about you?" Mrs. Hargrove offered the yams to Garrett who sat at Nicki's right.

"I've already had two helpings of yams." Garrett wondered why he'd avoided holiday dinners for so long. He kind of liked the friendly chaos of passing dishes and dodging elbows. He even tolerated Lester who sat to the left of Nicki, but who had the good sense to keep his mind on the food. "But thanks. I believe they were the best I've ever eaten."

Mrs. Hargrove beamed. "I put a little pineapple in them this year. It was a new recipe in *Woman's World*."

"I don't suppose you have the magazine with you?" Garrett had wondered how he could get his hands on a couple of issues. They were the experts at this male/female stuff and they should have an idea or two about how a man could propose after dinner with eighty other people around. At the very least, they should have a strategy for making sure Lester wasn't around when Garrett asked the big question.

Mrs. Hargrove looked over her shoulder. "I think Elmer took it to show to someone. But I don't see him. Unless he's over at table five."

The people at table number five all had their heads down studying something.

"There it is!" a boy whom Garrett didn't recognize said as he pointed. "That's got to be Boston." The boy looked up from the table and called over to Garrett. "Mister, have you been to Boston in that truck of yours?"

Garrett nodded. "I left the truck as close in as I could get at some delivery station and took a bus down to the Commons. I saw a boy skateboarding there about your size.''

''The maps were a brilliant idea,'' Mrs. Hargrove said. ''Everybody's been looking up cities and talking about traveling. Seems like everybody has a special place they want to see.''

Nicki was proud of Garrett. He'd answered everyone's questions about places he'd been and not made anyone feel foolish for asking anything, not even when Elmer had confused Rhode Island with Washington, D.C., on the map and asked if Garrett had shaken hands with the president there.

''Where would you go, Nicki?'' Mrs. Hargrove set the half-eaten dish of yams down. ''You haven't said yet.''

''She wants to see a whale,'' Garrett answered for her. ''I figure we should just drive over to Seattle and down the coast until we find one.''

''Why would she want to see a whale?'' Lester asked from Nicki's right. ''There are plenty of animals to see on the ranch.''

''I'm thinking of buying a book,'' Nicki added. ''That way I can see pictures of all kinds of animals.''

Garrett was wearing his tuxedo and Nicki had decided to wear a green pants suit that she kept for special occasions. She'd even put on some of the makeup Glory had lent her.

"A picture of a whale doesn't begin to do it justice," Garrett argued. He was glad he'd dropped the hint about taking Nicki down the coast. He figured he'd given everyone notice that way. But neither of the women even batted an eye over his statement and Lester just kept on eating. "I could drive you to see a whale in a day or two."

Lester did put down his fork at that.

"How nice." Mrs. Hargrove smiled politely.

Nicki didn't even bother to smile. "You're right. Maybe a video would be better than a picture."

"Are we going to have pie pretty soon?" Lester asked.

Garrett realized no one, not even Lester, thought he was serious about taking Nicki to see a whale. Either that or, he thought with dismay, they knew Nicki so well they were confident she would never go. If that was the case, his proposal was doomed.

Nicki wished Lester would forget about food for just one meal. How was her heart supposed to be happy at the prospect of a future with him when he seemed to care more about a piece of pie than he did about her? It wasn't that she was expecting love from Lester, she assured herself. Her feelings on that hadn't changed. She wanted a sound business relationship with him if he ever did propose. But she'd never expected to be less interesting to him than a piece of pie.

"I think there's going to be a little bit of a program before we have the pie," Mrs. Hargrove said. "It'll give everyone's meal time to settle."

"Oh," Lester said. "Then I think I'll have some more of the yams."

"I didn't know about a program." Nicki tried to keep the panic out of her voice.

"Well, 'program' is probably too formal of a word for it. The pastor was just going to say a few words—"

"Oh." Nicki relaxed.

"And then I think your mother was going to say something," Mrs. Hargrove continued.

"Oh." Nicki looked around to see how she could leave the bunkhouse. While all of the tables fit just fine when all of the chairs were pushed under the tables, when the chairs were pulled out and people were sitting in them, it was a different story. But she thought she could squeeze through to an outside aisle if she asked Mr. Jenkins to pull his chair over closer to Jacob's and lifted one of the Curtis twins up while she passed behind his chair.

Nicki stood up at the same moment that the pastor did. He had had the good sense to sit at the end of his table, however, so he wasn't caught in a sea of chairs like she was.

"Since this is truly a community Thanksgiving table," the pastor said, "our long-lost neighbor, Lillian

Redfern, has asked me to invite people to share what this community has meant to them.''

"Oh." Nicki sat back down.

Mrs. Hargrove was first. Then Mr. Lucas. Then Mr. Jenkins.

Nicki had decided her mother wasn't going to speak after all when her mother calmly stood up.

Lillian Redfern looked over the people in the room before she began to speak. As she looked, the room grew more and more silent. Finally, not even a fork was heard scraping against a plate.

"I came back to Dry Creek to say I am sorry I left twenty years ago. Charles and I were having problems and—well, it's not important what happened. He was angry with me. I was angry with him and swore it was all his fault. In the end, it didn't matter whose fault it was, I was the one who left. I didn't think about how many people my leaving hurt.''

Lillian looked directly at Nicki and Nicki lowered her eyes.

"Especially my children. I am very thankful to the people of Dry Creek for taking care of my children in my absence.'' Lillian swallowed and then continued. "The one thing I regret most in my life is that I lost my children. The one thing I am most grateful for is that I have been able to see them one more time.''

There was silence after Lillian sat down.

Nicki refused to look up from her plate. Her mother tied everything up in such a pretty little bow. Lillian might be able to fool the people of Dry Creek, but Nicki wasn't so easily fooled. She knew what her mother most regretted leaving behind.

Nicki looked up and over at her mother. "We have your china, you know."

"The china!" Lillian exclaimed excitedly as she stood up again and walked closer to Nicki's table. "Why didn't you say something? I thought something had happened to it."

"It's in the back closet," Nicki said. It was the only piece of her mother that still remained on the Redfern Ranch. Maybe it was time to let it all go. "I'm sure you'll want to take it back with you."

"Me?"

The surprise in her mother's voice made Nicki look up.

"Why, the china wasn't for me," Lillian said softly. "The china was always meant for you."

"What?"

Lillian nodded. "You were so taken with fairy tales as a child—remember how you used to always make a castle out of hay bales and play princess?"

"I outgrew fairy tales."

"I was sure you'd like those dishes in your own home someday. The rose pattern was so close to the border in your book on fairy tales. I was going to give the china to you when you got married.''

''Oh.'' Nicki remembered the roses. She still had the book on her bedroom bookcase. ''I thought it was all for you.''

Lillian shook her head and took a step closer to Nicki.

Chairs scraped and people moved until there was a path between Lillian and Nicki.

Nicki blinked her eyes, but she didn't move away. When her mother opened her arms, Nicki let herself be pulled into a hug.

''I'm so very sorry,'' her mother whispered into Nicki's hair. ''Can you forgive me?''

''I can try,'' Nicki replied. Maybe Garrett had been right and she should talk to the pastor. Maybe, if she asked for God's help, she could forgive her mother.

''That's all I ask.'' Nicki's mother held her.

''I didn't open the box,'' Nicki said as she pulled back a little from her mother's hug. ''But Dad packed them away carefully so they're probably still all right.''

''We'll wash them up for you and you can start using them.'' Lillian blinked a couple of times, as well.

Garrett sat at the table next to Nicki's empty chair and blinked his eyes, too. These holiday meals were nothing like he'd expected. He felt warm enough inside to hug someone himself. Garrett looked across Nicki's empty chair. There sat Lester eating his yams. Garrett drew the line at hugging Lester so, instead, he reached across the table and patted Mrs. Hargrove's hand. She took his hand in hers and squeezed it.

"Is it time for pie?" Lester looked up.

"I don't see why not," Mrs. Hargrove said as she stood. "They're on the table in the back, all cut and everything. If someone will help me pass them out, we'll get started."

Garrett helped Mrs. Hargrove pass out the pie slices. In the spirit of goodwill, he even brought Lester a second piece of pie after everyone else had been served.

"They got you trained," Lester sneered as he took the extra pie. "What are you going to do next—dishes?"

Garrett nodded. He figured he could take Lester in a fair fight. Maybe after he did the dishes would be a good time. "You going to stay around for a while?"

Lester nodded.

"Good."

Garrett looked up and saw Nicki leave the room with the Curtis twins. He supposed it was time for the promised ride on Misty.

Aunt Rose would love all this, Garrett thought to himself as he looked around in satisfaction. People had taken some of the tables down and sat around in small groups talking. A fire was going in the black cast-iron stove at one end of the bunkhouse and an electric heater was plugged in at the opposite end. The day outside was cold, but the sun was shining and someone had opened one of the windows.

"Hey, mister."

Garrett looked down to see the small boy who had asked him about Boston. Three other boys were with him.

"You want to play with us?" the boy asked. "We're going to play trucker."

Garrett smiled. "Maybe you'd like to see the inside of Big Blue."

"Can we?"

Garrett looked over to Mrs. Hargrove. "Don't start the dishes without me. I'll be back in ten minutes."

It was fifteen minutes before Garrett started walking back through the yard toward the house. The boys had been excited about all of the knobs and levers on Big Blue and Garrett had been distracted by the sight of Nicki outside leading Misty around the yard in a circle for the Curtis twins.

Nicki had put a parka over her pants suit and had taken off her shoes and put on her boots. The twins looked as though they were chattering and waving their arms trying to convince Misty to be a dragon. The mare just patiently kept walking. She did, however, obligingly lift her head periodically and blow out a gust of air that turned to fog in the cold afternoon air and could almost be mistaken for smoke. The twins giggled every time Misty did it.

''Hi,'' Garrett said as he walked up to them all.

''Do you think something's wrong with me?'' Nicki looked up from the ground and demanded of Garrett. When Nicki stopped walking, Misty stopped, too.

''No,'' Garrett answered firmly. Here was his chance. He could say he thought she was so wonderful that he wanted to drive away with her. Or that she was so perfect he wanted to marry her. Or that—

He didn't get a chance to say any of it.

''How can I promise to forgive someone when I don't know how I'll do it?'' Nicki asked.

''You'll have lots of help with that. The whole town will help, especially the pastor. He's already offered to help you sort it out. And, of course—'' Garrett took a deep breath ''—there's me. I'm happy to help.''

Garrett didn't know anything about forgiving someone, but he figured he could learn right along with Nicki. Maybe he could even learn about being committed to someone at the same time.

"How can you help?"

The horse nudged Nicki on the back. The twins were waving their arms around and shouting something about swords and fire.

"I could go to counseling with you." Garrett smiled. "I figure we've already aced marriage counseling. We make a good team in counseling."

The horse nudged Nicki again and she started leading the procession away. They'd gone a few yards when Nicki turned. "We flunked marriage counseling, you know."

"We were doing just fine. We only got through the first question." Garrett decided only a fool would propose to a women who was leading around a dragon being ridden by two little boys. But propose he would. He was working his way up to it. He just needed the right time and some romantic gesture.

Chapter Fourteen

Garrett stomped his shoes on the kitchen porch to make most of the snow drop off of them. He'd scrape them inside, too, after he took his jacket off. The air was much warmer inside the kitchen and Garrett stood in the entryway for a moment after he shut the door.

Garrett saw with satisfaction that a huge stack of dirty pots and pans sat on the counter by the sink. The soft sound of women's voices came from the living room.

He walked toward the voices. ''Thanks for not—''

''Oh.'' Lillian Redfern looked up and quickly snatched her blond wig back from Mrs. Hargrove. She put the wig on her head and looked up at Garrett. ''I was just—''

Garrett could see she wasn't finding the words to tell him what was wrong. "You don't have to explain. I just wanted to let you know I was going to go tackle those pots and pans." Garrett smiled. "That was a great meal you ladies put together," he said and turned to go.

"Wait." Mrs. Hargrove called him back. "Lillian, it's nothing to be ashamed of—you're going to have to tell people sooner or later." Mrs. Hargrove put her hand on Lillian's arm.

"You're right." Lillian nodded her head at Garrett. "Besides, you might be able to help Nicki understand when I tell her and Reno about it." Lillian took a deep breath. "The reason I lost my hair is because of the chemotherapy. I have breast cancer."

"And there's no reason to panic," Mrs. Hargrove said firmly. "My niece had breast cancer and she's made a nice recovery." She smiled at Lillian. "Her hair even grew back."

"I plan to tell Nicki and Reno this coming Sunday. I wanted them to get to know me a little more first," Lillian told Garrett. "So if you could keep it quiet for the time being."

"No problem. I wish you'd told me on the way up here though. I could have taken it easier and stopped in a hotel at night or something instead of just driving through like I did."

Lillian shook her head firmly. "Then we wouldn't

have made it in time for Thanksgiving. No, the reason I wanted you to drive me is because Chrissy said you'd be able to drive straight through. I wasn't up to flying, but I did want to get to Dry Creek for Thanksgiving.''

"I'm glad we made it for Thanksgiving, too," Garrett added softly.

Mrs. Hargrove looked at him. "I'm sure Nicki is happy you are here, too. You two seem to have hit it off.''

Garrett nodded. "I'll always remember Nicki.''

"Oh. You're leaving?" Mrs. Hargrove looked confused. "I thought you two were—well, maybe my old eyes aren't as sharp as they used to be.''

Garrett shook his head. "There's nothing wrong with your eyes. I plan to ask Nicki to marry me later today. I just don't think she'll say yes.''

"Oh." Mrs. Hargrove brightened. "Well, you don't know that until you ask, now do you?''

"I just wish I had some flowers.''

"There's an orchid in the refrigerator," Lillian suggested. "In some plastic box.''

"No, I think Nicki is more a roses kind of a woman. Even wild roses maybe." Garrett wondered if he could call a florist anywhere in the world and have roses delivered in the next few hours. "I don't suppose anyone grows roses around here and has one left in their garden.''

"It's freezing out there. The roses are all cut back." Mrs. Hargrove thought a moment. "You could make her a cowboy's rose though."

"What's that?"

"In the early days of the Redfern Ranch, a cowboy often gave his lady a rose made out of a folded bandanna. They actually found a way to fold them that made them look just like a rose."

"Nicki would like that." Garrett was encouraged. Anything to do with her ranch would please Nicki. "Where can I get a bandanna?"

"I'm sure her father had some," Lillian said as she stood up and adjusted her wig. "Let me run upstairs and check in the drawers. He always kept a package of brand-new ones in the top left drawer."

"Here, let me get them for you," Garrett offered as he motioned Lillian back to her seat.

"See." Lillian turned to Mrs. Hargrove. "That's why I don't like to tell people. Everyone treats me like an invalid." She turned to Garrett. "I'm perfectly able to climb a flight of stairs."

"I'm sure you are, ma'am."

Garrett watched Lillian walk toward the stairs. Why hadn't he noticed earlier that she was frail? That's probably why she'd been so quiet on the ride up here. "Do you think she'll be all right with Chrissy driving her back?"

Mrs. Hargrove nodded. "I'm sure they'll be fine."

"Well, I may as well get some of those pots in the dishwater so they can at least soak a few minutes." Garrett turned to leave for the kitchen.

"Good idea. Clear a place on the table so we can fold those bandannas."

The rose bandannas were easy to make and did look surprisingly like roses. Big, sturdy summer roses. "Now, you're sure Nicki will know what these are?"

Lillian nodded as she tied the roses together in a bouquet. "We used to make them when she was little. She'll remember."

Garrett hoped Nicki's mother was right. He was counting on the cloth roses to give his proposal respectability.

"You're welcome to use the ring, too." Lillian nodded her head toward the refrigerator. "I'd love for Nicki to wear it."

Garrett hesitated. "You know she's given me no reason to think she'll say yes?"

Lillian shrugged. "She seems to like you."

"But she's convinced that Lester is the man for her. And, to give the man his due, he does know about ranching and cattle. I only know about trucking. I don't see how I could make a living for Nicki and me here."

"Nicki would have to love you a lot to be willing to leave this ranch," Mrs. Hargrove agreed.

"That's why I'm saying I should leave the ring on the top of the refrigerator." Garrett felt the collar of his shirt grow tighter. He'd taken his tuxedo jacket off and rolled his sleeves up to do dishes. "What I'm doing is making a statement to Nicki. I don't think we can expect an engagement. I have Big Blue all packed and I intend to take off after she refuses me. To save everyone the awkwardness, you know."

"I see." Lillian smiled slightly. "Off into the sunset."

"The two of us can see to the last of these dishes," Mrs. Hargrove said. There was one last sinkful of pans still soaking. "But if you don't send me a Christmas card from wherever you are, I can tell you I'm going to be very disappointed."

Garrett looked at the two women. Aunt Rose would have approved. "I can do that."

"I saw Nicki go into the bunkhouse a little bit ago," Lillian added. "Reno is leading the horse around now."

"I don't think anyone else is in the bunkhouse," Mrs. Hargrove added. "We've been watching out the window. Last time I looked, I saw Lester talking with Mr. Jenkins over by the barn."

"Well—" Garrett rolled down the sleeves on his shirt and reached for his tuxedo jacket "—I guess there's no time like the present."

* * *

After Nicki had given the horse reins to Reno, she had gone into the bunkhouse.

The heat was fast leaving the bunkhouse, but the smell of turkey was still in the air everywhere except in the walk-in closet. The closet had obviously been added after the bunkhouse had been built and inferior lumber had been used. The slats didn't match properly and wind blew into the small room.

Nicki rubbed her arms. She'd taken her heavy coat off and laid it on the floor so she'd have something to sit on. Before that she had stopped to tie a full apron around her waist. She was grateful for the apron because no one had cleaned the closet for years and a film of dust had settled over everything. She'd also noticed water spots on the boxes so the roof in the closet must leak.

Nicki quietly sat cross-legged for a minute after she opened the flaps on the first box of china. Her father had wrapped each piece of china in newspaper, and Nicki slowly unwrapped a cup. It felt like her whole childhood came back to her. Her mother was right. Nicki did think of Cinderella fairy tales when she looked at the roses on those cups.

Last week Nicki would have sworn fairy tales were worthless and that it was best to live as though romance and flowers didn't exist. But now, she wondered if she'd just been afraid love would always disappoint her.

The door to the bunkhouse opened as Nicki took out another cup and unwrapped it. The older men sitting in the barn had come earlier to take a few folding chairs and they must want another one.

Garrett stood in the open doorway of the closet for a few moments just looking at Nicki. The white apron she wore was knee-length and it billowed out around her, as she sat with her legs folded under it. The wind had whipped her hair into disarray and it looked as if it was sprinkled with dust. He'd never seen a more beautiful woman.

"So this is the china?" Garrett walked over to where Nicki sat and got down on the floor himself. He had the rose bouquet in a brown paper bag that Mrs. Hargrove had given him.

Nicki looked over, smiled and nodded. "Silly, isn't it? What grown woman likes a china pattern because it reminds her of fairy tales?"

Garrett shrugged. "I can't think of a better reason."

"You know that pink dress we saw before—the one I thought my mother used to make me wear. I think I had it all wrong. I loved the dress. I used to pretend I was Cinderella."

"I rather like thinking of you as a princess."

"Oh, I stopped being a princess. All that feminine stuff—it's not me anymore. I gave up being pretty to be useful. I don't wear dresses anymore. It's all jeans. And boots.''

''Being feminine isn't about what you wear.''

Nicki smiled. ''I'm independent, too. I can milk a cow, change a tire, fix a tractor engine, do my taxes.''

''I get the picture,'' Garrett agreed. ''And none of that makes you any less of a princess. It's good that you can take care of yourself. I just think you should be cherished like a princess.''

Nicki blushed. ''You don't have to say that. I'm feeling a little better about my mother.''

''This isn't about your mother.'' Garrett didn't think his proposal was going very well. If he'd learned anything about women from his aunt Rose and Chrissy, it was that he shouldn't get involved in a mother/daughter problem. He needed to turn a corner here quickly.

''Well, I appreciate you trying to make me feel better anyway.'' Nicki smiled.

''I'm not trying to make you feel better.'' Garrett felt his voice rise in frustration. ''I'm trying to propose.''

''Oh.'' Nicki looked stunned. She jerked her head up so fast, some of the dust even fell out of her hair. ''To me?''

Garrett figured a proposal couldn't go much worse. ''Of course, to you.''

"Oh."

"I didn't mean for it to be so abrupt. I tried to give you a hint earlier with the whales."

"Oh."

Garrett thought Nicki looked a little white. "You're not going to faint on me, are you? If you hang your head down between your knees and take deep breaths, it will be all right."

Nicki closed her eyes. "That only works if you're sitting in a chair. I'll be fine. Just give me a minute."

"I've got all kinds of time."

Nicki took two deep breaths. "You mean marriage. You and me?"

"That was the general idea."

Nicki wondered when her world had gone crazy on her. She'd never expected to meet a man like Garrett. He could be in a fairy tale with all his talk of wanting to be a hero for his bride. A hero was a notch above a prince anyday.

Garrett had to talk. "I made you something—I know they're not real and you deserve ones that are real." He opened the bag and offered Nicki the bouquet of roses. "Your mother assured me you'd remember what these are."

"Cowboy roses," Nicki said softly as she accepted them. "They're perfect."

Nicki put the cloth roses up to her nose just as

though she could smell them. "I used to dream about cowboy roses."

"That's good then." Garrett decided things were going a little better. "Well, I just wanted you to know how I feel. I've never met anyone like you."

Nicki smiled. "I'm glad."

"And I want you to remember me," Garrett continued. "Even if you get married to Lester, I want you to remember me."

"I will."

Garrett looked at Nicki. He'd keep the picture of her eyes looking up at him in his heart forever. Quiet glowing emeralds. "I'll remember you, too."

"I'm going to kiss you now, so I don't want you to faint on me." Garrett leaned toward Nicki and she didn't move away.

A kiss can be about a million things, Nicki thought. But not every kiss made a woman feel as if she was a princess. It was too bad that every fairy tale didn't have a happy ending.

"I can't go with you," Nicki whispered finally.

"I know." Garrett drew her into his arms anyway.

"I need to be sensible."

"I know."

Garrett kissed her again. He was beginning to understand why the prince had been willing to search the whole kingdom for his princess. There would be no one else like Nicki in his life.

* * *

Mrs. Hargrove looked at Nicki's tearstained face. "Explain it to us again, dear."

Nicki had come running into the kitchen with tears streaming down her face. Lillian and Mrs. Hargrove had finished washing the last Thanksgiving pot and were having a cup of tea at the kitchen table.

"Life isn't like some fairy tale," Nicki said, and started to cry in earnest. "I have responsibilities. I can't just run off with any man who comes along who thinks I'm a princess."

"He thinks you're a princess?" Mrs. Hargrove said brightly. "That's a good sign."

"But I have chores to do," Nicki wailed. "I can't fall in love."

"Well, someone else can do the chores," Lillian said as she leaned in to hold her daughter. "That's no reason to stay."

Nicki stopped crying and hiccuped. She pulled away from her mother's reach. "I'm not like you. I keep my commitments."

Lillian sat back in her chair. "I see."

"Dear, I hope you're not talking about a commitment to Lester," Mrs. Hargrove said. "I'm not sure he's the right man for you."

"I'm not talking about Lester. Well, not much. I mean the land. I'm committed to the Redfern Ranch. Dad gave it to me and Reno. He meant for me to stay.'' Nicki dried her eyes and looked at her mother. ''I'm not going to leave everything like you did.''

Nicki sat up straighter in her chair. She was a strong woman. She had her land. She had her boots. She could do what needed to be done in life.

''Oh, dear, is that what you think?'' Lillian finally spoke. ''That you need to stay because I left?''

''Dad was never the same after you left. He loved you and you left him. I've learned a person can't count on love, but the land stays with you.''

There was silence in the kitchen.

''Lillian, you have to tell her what happened,'' Mrs. Hargrove finally said as she rose from the table. ''I'll go wait in the living room so you have some privacy.''

''You don't need to leave.'' Nicki smiled at Mrs. Hargrove. ''She doesn't need to tell me anything. I know what happened.''

''No,'' Mrs. Hargrove said as she stood up. ''You don't.''

Lillian waited for Mrs. Hargrove to walk into the living room. ''Do you want some tea?''

Nicki shook her head. ''What does Mrs. Hargrove mean? You left Dad—that's all there is to it.''

Lillian shook her head. ''What Mrs. Hargrove wants me to tell you is why I left. I'm still not sure it is a good idea. And I'm not saying that it excuses my leaving. If I'd had as much character as you have,

I would have stayed and worked the situation out. But I just didn't know what to do but leave.''

"Dad said you left to pursue your dancing career.''

Lillian smiled wryly. "That's what I did, but that's not why I left.'' Lillian looked down at her hands. "Do you remember Betty, Jacob's wife?''

"Of course. The two of them used to be over here all the time.''

Lillian nodded. "Betty and your father were having an affair.''

"What?''

"I didn't believe it when Jacob first told me, but then I asked your father and he admitted it.''

"Jacob knew?''

"He knew. Mrs. Hargrove knew. And Elmer. Except for Betty and your father, that was all. I left the day after he admitted it to me. Jacob asked us all to keep it quiet because he was fighting to save his marriage.''

"I never knew. I thought you left because you didn't like me anymore,'' Nicki said.

"Never,'' Lillian said as she leaned toward Nicki to give her a hug.

This time Nicki didn't move away.

"Don't give up on love if he's the one you want,'' Lillian whispered into Nicki's hair. "Don't make my mistake. If you love him, you can work it out.''

''But he moves all over and I stay in one place.''

Lillian smiled. ''You've never heard of compromise? Maybe you could move a little and he could stay a little.''

Nicki frowned a minute then smiled. ''That doesn't sound so hard.''

Lillian kissed her daughter on the forehead. ''It won't be. Now go. I heard the truck start up ten minutes ago.''

''He's leaving?''

Nicki stood and started walking toward the kitchen door. She grabbed a coat off the rack before she opened the door and went outside. Even when she shaded her eyes with her hand, Nicki could barely see the truck down the road. It was a dot disappearing on the white horizon.

She slipped the coat on over her pants suit and started running toward the barn. The keys were in the pickup. Nicki opened the side door to the barn and stopped. The pickup stood where it always did, right in front of the double doors that led outside. But it wasn't going to be easy to move it. Several of the older men from dinner had set their folding chairs around the truck. Someone—Nicki thought it might be Jacob—was even taking a nap in the back of the pickup.

Nicki turned around and walked out of the barn. It would be easier to take Misty.

"Sorry," Nicki said as she helped the last of the twins down from the saddle. "I'll bring her back in a few minutes."

"She blows smoke in the air," one of the twins announced. "I think she can fly."

The other twin nodded. "She just doesn't want to fly because she's afraid she'll scare the chickens. That's what Reno says."

"You can get the kids to the house all right?" Nicki asked Reno and Chrissy who had been leading Misty around in circles until Nicki came.

"Of course." Reno looked offended. "They're my pals."

Nicki swung herself up into the saddle. Some days it paid to wear boots. She turned Misty around and nudged the mare with her knees.

Misty gave a happy snort and galloped for the gate.

Nicki kept her head down and her collar pulled up. The wind had a bite to it, but it also smelled fresh. A few sprinkles of snow were falling. Nicki watched as the gray and white clumps of ground sped past Misty's feet. Nicki looked up once to see Garrett's truck. She wondered what he was thinking.

Garrett was beginning to wish he'd taken his swing at Lester when the man had stepped out of the barn as Garrett was walking back to his truck. Instead, Garrett had shaken the man's hand and confused him by congratulating him. Not that hitting Lester would change anything, Garrett told himself, but he was itching to do something.

Garrett decided he should have had real flowers. Maybe when he got into Miles City he could stop at a florist and ask them to deliver a bouquet of roses to Nicki. Just so she'd know he wanted her to have them.

From Miles City, he would head out to—Garrett realized he didn't care where he headed out to. He'd already been most of the places he'd ever hoped to see—some of them four or five times.

Still, he had the freedom to go anywhere he wanted.

Yeah, he thought as he turned on his truck's radio, he might be unlucky in love, but he was a lucky man because he could drive Big Blue anywhere his heart desired.

What was wrong with him? Garrett thought to himself. He didn't have the freedom to go where he wanted. The only place his heart wanted to go was five miles behind him and he was headed away from it with every turn of Big Blue's tires. What kind of luck was that?

The road Garrett was driving down was a country dirt road with shallow ditches between it and lines of barbed-wire fence. Cows watched him as he drove by, and the road was narrow. There was no place to turn around until he came to the main road a couple of miles ahead of him.

Garrett pressed a little harder on the gas pedal.

Nicki thought she'd never catch Garrett. Just when she thought she'd make it, he sped up as if he was in some kind of a race. She wondered if he saw her in the rearview mirror. She probably looked a sight, like a madwoman, with her coat flapping about her as she and her horse charged after him. She'd been trying to tell him she wasn't a princess—at least now he might believe her.

Garrett blinked. He saw a flash of green in his mirror and then he hit a bump and the vision vanished. He craned his neck to get a better look. He was catching glimpses of a cape or a jacket flapping in the wind. His best guess was that something was following directly behind him and a piece of cloth was flapping about. He strained his neck even farther. He should be able to see if it was a car. But it was something thinner than a car. A bicycle couldn't go that fast so it must be some kid on a motorcycle.

Garrett slowed down. He had no desire to race a kid on a motorcycle on Thanksgiving Day in the cold and snow. He'd let the kid pass him.

Garrett pulled the truck over to the edge of the road and stopped. He checked the mirror to see how far back the motorcycle was and saw it wasn't a motorcycle at all. It was Misty. And Nicki.

Garrett rolled down his window. The wind was gusty and more snow flurries were beginning to fall.

Nicki reined Misty in. Finally. She and Misty were both breathing hard and their breath was making clouds around their faces. But they were here.

Oh, no, Nicki thought. They were here. She'd concentrated so hard on catching up with Garrett that she hadn't thought of what to say to him when she actually caught up with him.

''You left,'' she accused him. The wind carried Nicki's words away and she leaned closer to yell inside Garrett's truck. ''I didn't know you were going to leave.''

''I said goodbye.'' Garrett wondered if the sun had come out from behind a cloud. Even with the wind and the snow, the day seemed warmer and brighter than before.

''Well, you should have told me you were leaving. And you didn't get any leftover pie,'' Nicki yelled into the truck, her hands cupped around her mouth.

''Oh.'' Had he heard right? The day dimmed again. He rolled his window completely down. ''You came to bring me pie?''

''Well.'' Even in the cold, Nicki felt her face flush. She took a deep breath. ''No, I forgot the pie.''

''That's okay. Tell Lester he can have my piece.''

Nicki forced herself to take another breath and then she spoke loudly. "I came about the whale. You said you'd take me to see a whale."

Garrett knew now why a deaf man would sing. He leaned out the door window and felt the bite of snow on his skin. It could have been a caress. "You don't need to go anywhere you don't want to go. I was going to turn around when I got up to the country road."

Nicki wasn't sure she had heard all of that. "You were coming back?" Nicki straightened herself on her horse. "Did you forget something?"

Garrett leaned out the window so he could see Nicki's face. The wind had whipped her hair around her head and put red blotches on her face. "I forgot you. You're my princess."

Nicki started to grin. The man was completely blind. "A princess would have waited at the castle for her hero to come back."

"Not in my fairy tale," Garrett said as he leaned far enough out of his window to kiss Nicki.

Epilogue

Nicki hated to admit it, but her mother was right. Compromise did make everything possible.

When Nicki admitted to Garrett that she had always wanted rose petals to line her bridal path, he swore that's what she'd have even though she had added that she didn't need them. She knew there wouldn't be enough roses in Dry Creek until Mrs. Hargrove's flowers started to bloom in June.

"June!" Garrett had sounded stunned when she told him that. Then he swallowed. "I didn't know it would be that long, but if that's what you want, that's what we'll do."

Nicki smiled. "There's nothing so special about roses. Maybe I could have carnations or something. Then we could get married in February."

"Carnations don't have any smell, but I like the sounds of February. We'll ask Matthew if the church is available."

"Matthew said any time we picked, he'd make sure it was available."

Nicki was surprised how much her feelings about the Dry Creek church had changed. She'd grown up in that church, but it wasn't until she forgave her mother that she was able to feel God's love wrap around her. Now she felt that love every time she walked into the church. She wouldn't want to be married in any other place.

Garrett seemed to feel the same way.

"If I'm going to be the kind of husband to you that I want to be, I'm going to need God's help," Garrett had told her one Sunday after dinner. They were sitting together on the sofa in the living room at the Redfern Ranch.

He was silent for a moment.

"I had no idea God cared about me the way He does," Garrett finally added.

"I know what you mean," Nicki said. She used to think God didn't care about the Redfern family, but now she saw His blessings everywhere.

Earlier that day, they had walked around the site of the home they were building on the other side of the bunkhouse. Garrett had pulled enough money out of his savings account to pay for the complete three-bedroom house.

Nicki had never thought she could have her own home and stay on the ranch, as well. But then, Nicki was looking forward to many things she'd never thought she could have.

For their honeymoon trip, Nicki wanted to take a trip with Garrett in Big Blue.

"We've got the bed right in back," Garrett reminded her and winked. "In case we want a nap."

"We won't make it out of Dry Creek if all we do is sleep."

Garrett leaned over to hug Nicki. Garrett never thought he'd know the kind of contentment he had these days. Maybe half of his desire to see new places was just a way of looking for a community. Now that he'd found that community, he didn't need to keep looking.

"But I still want to see the ocean." Nicki sighed as she felt Garrett's arms wrap around her.

Garrett wondered if the compromise he and Nicki had made had flipped them both around. They had agreed that Garrett would make short hauls during the winter months to make money and then help around the ranch during the rest of the year. Nicki had done the financial calculations and figured they'd double the income of the ranch that way. Garrett was happy with the arrangement and was discovering he liked the time best when he was on the ranch.

Nicki, on the other hand, was sending away for travel brochures and making her list of places she wanted to see.

"You promised me the ocean," Nicki whispered with her head snuggled on Garrett's chest.

"That's just the beginning," Garrett agreed as he hugged her even closer.

Their wedding took place on Sunday, February 1, at two o'clock in the afternoon. But the people of Dry Creek swore they would remember the day before even more than the wedding day itself.

"I'll think of that big truck every time I smell a rose," Mrs. Hargrove said. "Why, the whole town smelled like roses."

Garrett had driven Big Blue down to Los Angeles to pick up his aunt for the wedding. While he was there, he'd gone to the flower mart and bought a hundred dozen red roses.

"That's twelve hundred roses," Mrs. Hargrove told the men at the hardware store when she went inside to get out of the cold. "You should have seen Nicki's face when he opened up the back of the truck and those flowers fell out. She's still out there—just standing with Garrett in the middle of the roses."

For once the men were speechless, except for Lester who gave a low whistle of admiration before saying, "He's some guy, that Garrett."

Mrs. Hargrove glanced out the window. "She's going to get cold."

Mrs. Hargrove saw Garrett open his arms and enclose Nicki in them. "Well, maybe not so cold, after all."

Nicki knew it was cold. If was, after all, February in Montana. "You didn't need to do that."

"I know." Garrett smiled as he looked down at Nicki. The cold had turned her cheeks pink and her lips white. She was beautiful.

Nicki swore she could feel rose petals through the soles of her boots. Their perfume drifted up to her as she gazed at her very own prince. She wondered why she'd ever been so set against fairy tales. "You're sparkling."

"It must be snowing."

* * * * *

Dear Reader,

I started this book with the image of a snow globe in my mind. As the characters in the book grew, I realized the image of looking through thick snow was the feeling that Nicki must have had in her life. Because she had not forgiven her mother, she had not been able to fully see the hope for love that she had as a woman. It was as though falling snow hid this hope from her sight, and she only caught glimpses of it in her dreams.

I believe the same is true for each of us. When we do not forgive others, we limit ourselves. Forgiveness is not always easy. In fact, it can sometimes seem impossible. The miraculous thing is that God is able to change our hearts and help us forgive. And by doing so, we gain freedom ourselves.

God bless us all as we seek to forgive each other.

Yours always,

Janet Tronstad

If you enjoyed
A HERO FOR DRY CREEK,
you'll love the next book
in Janet Tronstad's DRY CREEK miniseries:
A BABY FOR DRY CREEK

Available February 2004
for a sneak peek, turn the page....

Prologue

Forty years ago, the families of the ranches outside of the town of Dry Creek, Montana, put up a row of metal boxes beside the hardware store so that the mail carrier could leave their mail there on his way east to the county line. Over the years these boxes got battered by hailstorms and bleached by the sun until the mail carrier could no longer read which name went with which box.

Now the mail carrier just leaves everyone's mail on the counter next to the cash register inside the hardware store. The method works well, and there's never been any problem until the day a letter arrived in an ivory envelope with the name of a California legal firm embossed in the upper left-hand corner. The letter was addressed to ''The Postmaster at Dry Creek, Montana.''

J. M. Price, Attorney-at-law
918 Green Street, Suite 200
Pasadena, California 91104

Dear Dry Creek Postmaster,

I'm writing to request your help in locating a man who lives in your community. Unfortunately, I do not know the man's full name so I can not write to him directly. The nature of my business is this man's relationship with a young woman named Chrissy Hamilton, and her new baby. It is the paternity of the infant that I wish to establish.

Miss Hamilton was in your community last fall. I am hopeful you will know the young man who spent the night with Miss Hamilton in her cousin's truck. The man's first name is Reno. If you can supply me with the man's full name, I assure you my client, Mrs. Bard, will be happy to reward you (you have no doubt heard of the family—they own the national chain of dry cleaners by the same name). I realize this is an unusual request and I want to assure you that no one is asking the man to assume financial responsibility for the baby. Quite the opposite, in fact. Mrs. Bard is anxious to adopt the baby should it be proven to her satisfaction that her son, Jared, is the baby's father. I apologize for the unorthodox nature of this request. It would not be necessary if Miss Hamilton were more cooperative. But she is young (eighteen, I believe) and does not yet see the full advantage to herself in this arrangement. I look forward to hearing from you soon.

Yours truly,
Joseph M. Price, Esq.